TAC LEADER

#2

Night Hawks

Books by Bob Anderson

Sarge, What Now?
Grandfather Speaks
Anderson's Rules

TAC Leader Series

#1: What Honor Requires
#2: Night Hawks
#3: Retribution

Books by Jerry Ahern, Sharon Ahern
and
Bob Anderson

The Survivalist Series

#30: The Inheritors of Earth
#31: Earth Shine
#32: The Quisling Covenant
The Shades of Love (Short Story)
Once Upon a Time (Short Story)
Light Dreams (Short Story)

Rourke Chronicles
#1: Everyman

**For more exciting
Books, eBooks, Audiobooks and more visit us at
www.speakingvolumes.us**

TAC LEADER

#2

Night Hawks

Bob Anderson

SPEAKING VOLUMES, LLC
NAPLES, FLORIDA
2015

#2 Night Hawks

Editing assistance provided by Pamela Anderson.

ISBN 978-1-61232-941-3

Dedication

To all of those brave people who every day climb out of bed to struggle and fight against the apathy of the masses and the greed of a few. To those brave men and women who elect to place themselves in harm's way to protect those around them; each of them is a hero.

To my wife Pam; my partner, my lover, my friend and one of the bravest people I know. To those who keep on doing the right thing—even when it is hard to do so. To those who keep speaking the truth—even when it is hard to do so.

Remember what Gandhi said, "Just because you are the only voice in the forest does not mean you are wrong." Bravery is not the absence of fear; it is heroic deeds done in the presence of fear. No Retreat—No Surrender!

Acknowledgments

Special thanks go out to Janet Robbins—a devoted fan, and Kim Kuri—a valuable resource who worked graciously and diligently for Doc and the team. Also thanks to Mike Robinson and Heidi Lee of BlackHawk Paramotor for technical guidance, Jeff Knox of Knox Knives, Pat and Wes Crawford of Crawford Knives, Tom and Katie Kulwicki, and Keith Roosa of Allesi Holsters. Lastly, thanks to Mike Stadelmaier.

Question: "What do you call people who when faced with a fearful situation, do nothing?"

Answer: "Civilized?"

— Dialogue between Charles Bronson's character and his son-in-law from the movie "*Death Wish*." This was following a vicious attack on his wife and daughter, that left the wife dead and the daughter terribly injured.

Prologue

The man sat next to the open side of his three-sided "Mayan" fire pit; the open flame highlighting his face. The walls, almost two feet high, were constructed of broken blocks of concrete. Behind the back wall of the pit where he had stacked red landscape blocks up in a pyramid design, on top sat a sculptured bust of a Cheyenne Dog Soldier. It looked as though he was staring into the Dog Soldier's eyes, but the truth was he didn't see the bust or the fire. In fact, he didn't even see the fire pit.

It was hot in Houston, Texas and he didn't need the fire for warmth. There was something soothing in the flames, almost like watching the oceans waves break on a beach. It often amazed him that he received the same peace of mind whether he was watching fire or water.

Wearing a pair of moccasins and walking shorts, his chest was bare. His sweaty and scarred torso bore witness that he had recently been through hell. The wounds were healed now, the scars were still visible. He still felt an occasional twinge in those places, but he had been declared fit for duty.

He was lost in the memories of battle. As he stared ahead, it played again in his memory.

He knew he was going to die before he made the leap. In slow motion, he saw the cylinder of the 12-gauge Street Sweeper index the next round, saw the fire belch out of the barrel and felt the buck shot slam into him. He felt himself flying backwards and slam into the ground;

he felt the darkness pass over him and felt himself slip into what he thought was death.

His hands clenched and his chest hurt; badly. He rubbed his fist across his chest as the vision slowly receded from his mind. He came back to reality with a start; he was still in a lawn chair beside the Mayan fire pit. He reached down and picked up his drink from the table sitting next to him, took a sip of Jack Daniels Old Number Seven and wiped his face and body off with a dirty t-shirt. He held his hands out and watched them continue to shake. It was over for now but he wondered if the vision would ever stop coming.

Doc Roberts stood up and headed for the bathroom and mumbled, "Here we go again. I am getting entirely too old for this shit. I wonder if it is true that every saint has a past and every sinner has a future." It was time to finish packing; the cruise started tomorrow.

Chapter One
The Present—April 1999

I was sitting comfortably on a chair in our state room looking out the glass door to the balcony. I watched the sun slowly sink below the crimson clouds on the western horizon while Pam made the last touches on her makeup and hair for the evening.

The boat was a big one. I guess it was big enough to be called a ship; however, since I was never in the Navy, I was blessed with not having to worry about such things. Damned thing was a boat to me. The smell of sea air and the smell of air in the high mountains share a similar quality, although the fragrances are completely different. That quality is openness. In the high mountains, the line of sight is usually vertical. I could see all the way to heaven and most of the way to hell. The cruise ship was headed to Cozumel.

At sea it is different—line of sight is horizontal and empty for as far as you can see in any direction. After just a few hours, you can see neither where you came from nor where you're going. In fact, where you are looks exactly like where you were thirty minutes ago, and where you'll be thirty minutes from now. In that aspect, it reminded me of the north Mexican desert we had been in just a few short weeks ago. I was still recuperating, the stitches were out, the bruises and scars were fading, and my strength and endurance was almost back to normal. Except for the dream, I was "marvelous, simply marvelous," to quote Billy Crystal.

Probably the dream would come back again tonight, as it had every night for the last two weeks. The shrink calls it Traumatic Memory Manifestation; I call it bullshit. I should have been toast, and would have been were it not for the trauma shock plates in my tactically rated bullet-resistant vest. I call it bullet resistant; nothing is ever truly "bulletproof."

The .33 caliber lead slugs slammed into the trauma plate; they smashed the plate all to hell and then skittered across my chest, into my neck, both arms and other body parts. In their erratic path, ripping large and uncomfortable grooves across my chest and shoulders, were several holes through which I managed to lose almost fifty percent of my blood volume. Now, after just a few weeks, I felt mostly healed; I'd feel even better when, and if, the dream stopped.

My name is Marv Roberts, but everyone calls me "Doc." I had taken some guys I knew, mounted a successful penetration into Mexico and successfully rescued a group of hostages and victims who ranged in age from ten years old to early twenties. With monies we had "liberated" from the bad guys, we created the Blue Feather Foundation to administer funds necessary for the medical, psychological and sociological rehabilitation of those victims.

We hadn't been concerned about prosecution or arrest; we just did what was necessary to fix a problem. Yeah, we did it rather explosively with a definite note of finality, but we hadn't embarrassed anyone—in other words, we didn't drawn attention to either government. Those government types had appreciated the fine line we had drawn.

My old friend and former boss, David A. Blaine, had retired as Chief of Security Police for 15th Air Force, after a stellar military career. He was what the Air Force called a "fast burner," a super troop, and had made a name for himself as a troubleshooter; a fixer.

When he arrived at an Air Force Base that had problems, he'd fix them. Most of his career was spent with Air Force Security Police, earning six Outstanding Unit Awards and two Best in the Air Force Trophies, not to mention a chest full of medals and ribbons from this country as well as the governments of several of our allies. He was a former Deputy Chief for Counter Terrorism for USAFE, the United States Air Forces Europe.

Blaine knew how to keep his mouth shut and had proven it. He had proven he knew how to get the job done. David Blaine was, in my opinion, the closest thing to King Arthur, the ideal leader, I have ever seen. That I had only worked for him about two years, and that was over twenty years ago, did not reduce that serious endorsement. At the end of our last mission, he made an offer that we accepted; the TAC Team was now sanctioned. David served as Liaison and Chief Operating Officer.

A knock at the door jolted me back to the present. I walked to the door and opened it; my son, John Roberts, was standing there in his tuxedo. "Aren't you guys ready yet?" he asked.

"Warlord," I said, "you have your clothes on, I have my clothes on, but neither of our women is ready so let's just have a beer and relax."

"That's one of the things I like about you, Dad," he grinned. "You have a marvelous ability to observe a situation, analyze the nature of the condition and identify the most appropriate response. Give me a Miller." A half of a beer later, Pam appeared.

"Wow!" I said.

"Yeah, wow," John agreed.

Pam's dress was black; she favored black and black favored her. It was form-fitted and sequined with a slit up the leg. A single strand of pearls was around her neck; simply eloquent, simply beautiful. With a gentle rap on the door that joined the two state rooms, Beth stepped in to our room. Her dress was midnight blue and she was a vision.

John said, "Wow!"

"Yeah, wow," I agreed. I handed him his beer and picked up my own. "Here's to us, Bud; the two luckiest guys on this boat with the two prettiest ladies on this boat."

"It's a ship, you idiot," he said, then raised his glass, "but I will go along with the rest of the sentiments. To you, ladies."

We toasted them and arm in arm, we headed for the ballroom and the evening show and banquet. I watched John and his wife and it pleased me, it was good to see him happy. Not just functional; not just content, but happy.

I turned to watch Pam. Lately, she had insisted on wearing her hair short, damned near as short as mine. I am still old fashioned enough to enjoy long hair on a woman; but what the hell, she'd look good bald— I think, but I really did not want to go there.

She can be a demanding wench; she actually thinks that it's necessary for me to be looking at her for us to talk. She can't get it through her head that I've been trained to pay attention to several things simultaneously and respond appropriately to all of them. I do what all of we advanced life forms do when it comes to women; I capitulate and do as I'm told.

It's amazing how different male and female Homo sapiens are. It really is as though we sprang up on separate planets. But I know she is good for me and *that* makes me want to be better for her.

We entered the ballroom and for the next two hours watched a magician, a comedian and then were entertained by a Torch Light singer accompanied on the Grand Piano. I glanced over at John and stood. He raised his glass of Crown and Coke and I saluted with my Jack and Seven. "To us and those like us," I said.

"Damned few left," he responded and we both took a swig. The last song was one of my favorites, a rendition of Lou Rawls' famous, "*You'll Never Find a Love Like Mine*." We escorted our ladies to the dance floor for a song that *demands* a dance with your special lady. At the end of the dance, John and Beth headed back to the state room. Pam and I walked around the deck. The night breeze was cool and the moon was dancing on the still ocean, creating an ivory carpet from the side of the ship to the edge of the horizon. I reached in my pocket and took out a container I had purchased that day in the ship's gift shop.

"What's that?" Pam asked.

"Insurance," I said, smiling. I unscrewed the top and poured about half of the container in my hand and checked the wind. "Make a wish," I told her. She shut her eyes, then opened them and nodded. I waved my hands and arms around and mumbled some Latin phrases; well at least they sounded Latin to me. I opened my hand and sprinkled the wind. Gold, pink and green flashes caught the lights of the ship, the light of the moon and the lights from Pam's eyes.

"Pixie Dust," she giggled. "That means my wish will come true."

"You can count on it," I said, "you can count on it." I dusted the glitter... pixie dust, off my hands and took her in my arms. I kissed her and said again, "You can count on it." Music drifted out of the salon as we passed and I spun her around on the deck. We danced slowly to Carly Simon's *"Time After Time."* The night was perfect and so was she.

Chapter Two

The next day, we did the tourist bit in Cozumel. Though dark clouds were brewing in the distance, the weather couldn't have been better. The girls shopped; John and I carried their loot. Not the best arrangement possible, but the only one we were offered. We spent the morning looking for the best deals. Haggling over prices was part of the process; initially Pam was not comfortable with it.

Beth had it down to an art, and by mid-morning Pam had become an excellent haggler. I knew then we had created a monster. We carried the loot to the Lagoon Cafe and had a light lunch. Not a bad way to spend an afternoon and the night would prove to be equally delightful.

After breakfast the next day, we left the ship on a ferry and booked a bus for the interior; I was about to see the Mayan temples. The boat ride had been exciting and refreshing, the cool sea spray invigorating. The bus ride, to my surprise, was not bad. The seats were cushioned and the air conditioner actually worked... a little at least.

The sights and smells in town reminded me of my tour in the Philippines, until we got into the countryside.

All of my life I had imagined the area to be jungle, like Tarzan's home and like what I had seen in the Philippines. It wasn't; the vegetation in this area is more like a short forest, the trees seldom get over twelve feet tall and the area is dry and dusty. Several things became evident: Number one, it was hot; number two, it was dusty; number three, the ride was bumpy but the beer was cold and there was a lot of it.

By the time we arrived at Tulum, the only walled city of the Mayans, we were relaxed, more than slightly buzzed and ready to stretch our cramped muscles. It is difficult to describe this lost city that had been rediscovered and redeveloped by man. The avenues, vistas and parks had been created by a lost and dead civilization. When it was rediscovered, the jungle had been forced back, re-exposing the terraces and promenades.

The buildings and structures were now empty, except for the passing of tourists and the iguanas that inhabited them. Once they had pulsed with the life of the city—songs, laughter, talk, noise, barking of dogs, chatter of monkeys, and the other sounds of people going on about their daily business.

Now, a strange hush settled over the entire panorama. We unconsciously lowered our voices and restrained ourselves rather than disturb the ghosts and memories of this place. I knew a little of the history of this region and the people that built this city. Their descendants still lived in the region, but not in the glory of their forefathers.

This civilization had peaked and died when the Spanish arrived.

Although a literate people with a highly developed form of written language, little is known of the ancient Maya today. During the "process of Christian civilization," Catholic missionaries burned almost all of the Mayan codicils. These were extensive "books" laboriously written on pages of wood—they covered the entire history and culture of the Mayans.

It seems that cruelty, murder and even genocide were necessary for the success of Christian civilization.

The pyramid tour was educational but somewhat depressing. Something about walking around in a dead city and trying to imagine it full of people bothered me.

The bus trip back quickly perked up my spirits. The beer was no longer cold, but there was still plenty of it. I saw John talking to one of the other travelers we had met, a slightly overweight chiropractor with a winning smile and a sharp mind named Jerry Ferris. Going for another beer for each of the girls and myself, I made my way to the back of the bus to the ice chests and passed John and Jerry. Ferris was excited and talking in animated but subdued tones. Obviously, he had John's attention. I thought, *Hmmm, I think Warlord has made contact.*

Blaine had told me that this was to be a "working vacation" and one of us needed to gain some independent Intel on what might be our next TAC Team mission; only God and Blaine knew what this one would be.

Loaded up with the beers in hand, I started back. The bus was filled with loud laughter, singing and other sounds of good fun. The bus bounced down the rutted dirt and gravel road, finally rolling into the parking area for the tour service. Returning to the waterfront, we gathered our loot and headed for the ferry that brought us back to the ship. The breeze created by our movement through the water helped blow away some of the dust that collected from our bus ride.

Hot, dirty, and a little tipsy, but still functional, John pulled me to one side and glanced around to make sure only the girls were close enough to hear. "Guess what?" he said, smiling.

"What?"

"Our friend," he nodded toward Jerry, "has a friend of a friend who arranged for a special party for him. He says it's a preview for a new place opening outside of Baton Rouge, in the River Parishes area."

"So?" I said.

"So, the place will be called The Willows Resort."

My interest peaked. "Could this be a sexually oriented business by any chance?"

"You got it! The place is by invitation only, the clientele restricted to those enjoying the 'ultimate in alternative pleasure seeking.' You have to have one of these to even get in," he said, and handed me a card. It said simply "The Willows Resort" and gave a phone number, but it was the logo that caught my eye. It was the same logo that had been on the medallion Val Richards wore and embroidered on the jogging suits he provided to his guests.

I pocketed the card and said, "When is this place supposed to open?"

"Jerry said within the month." John smiled. "I think we need to contact Mr. Blaine, don't you?" John handed me some Polaroid snapshots. "This is who they're swinging with," he said, in disgust. The pictures were of kids in a variety of sexual poses.

"Yes, yes I do," I said. "Tell him we can't do the party, the girls are not into it, but tell him that you and I are interested and want to learn more. Let's get as much information as we can. I'll call Blaine when we get back to Houston."

John nodded.

Chapter Three

By the time we docked on U.S. soil, Jerry Ferris was convinced that he had found two like-minded cohorts in John and me. We convinced Ferris that we would be most interested in joining him at The Willows for some "recreation." We shook hands as we came down the gangway with promises of "see ya soon."

Pam and I collected our bags and said "adios" to John and Beth, who headed back home. On our way back to Houston, Pam and I discussed the situation and were developing plans.

Hank Devlin and I had stumbled onto Val Richards' operation by accident, but what we had done to disrupt his operation had not been an accident. It was planned and coordinated with vision and forethought, and not without malice. I won't bore you with the details.

Suffice it to say, some "creative financing" had funded the activation of the TAC Team and now, as a result of that operation, we had become a group of unofficial and anonymous individuals whose function was to handle what conventional authorities could not, or would not, handle.

Our function was to "fix the unfixable and to repair that which cannot be repaired." Our job was to do what no one else could, or would, do.

Val's operation had been part of vast underground criminal organization that appeared to be resurfacing. This time it was operating on American soil, in the swamps and bayous of South Louisiana. It was a sophisticated new twist on an old criminal activity.

It was prostitution carried to the next level; the level of white slavery. Now, another head of this dragon was rearing up and roaring and would soon be belching fire; that is unless someone stopped it…more specifically, unless we stopped it.

When we arrived home, I called Blaine. His instructions were succinct and specific. I was to head to Baton Rouge, Louisiana and start digging for more information now that we had a lead.

Chapter Four

If you haven't been there, I can tell you Louisiana is a unique place. I was raised in the northwest corner of the state in a city called Shreveport. Northwest Louisiana more nearly resembles East Texas than the rest of Louisiana, in that it is predominately conservative, protestant and Republican.

I had moved to Baton Rouge in 1990 and learned that south Louisiana was so different I began calling it the 51st state. More accurately, Louisiana could be called two states and a foreign country all rolled into one political entity.

The city of Alexandria in central Louisiana, or Alex as the locals call it, is the point of demarcation. South of Alex, the state is historically Democratic, ultraliberal and Roman Catholic. Between Baton Rouge, New Orleans and Thibodeaux are the River Parishes. By my reckoning, this is almost a separate country, barely even America.

The French influence is remarkable. Witness, for example, that all other states have counties—only Louisiana has parishes and Louisiana has laws still based on the Napoleonic Code. The history of the area reflects Indian, French, Spanish and English influences.

Racial boundaries in many families have been blurred over the years. *"Les Bon Temps Roulette"*, Let the Good Times Role, is the official and unofficial battle cry of south Louisiana. This area has industrial centers that service the entire country. It is also a cultural center whose impact is felt across the south; yet, there is a dark side also. Alcoholism and drug use is common; likewise, so are domestic violence and sexual incest.

Some of the finest chefs and jazz in the world call Louisiana home. South Louisiana is often a contradiction. Mudbugs, filet, Étouffée and gumbo exist side by side with Exxon, Texaco and other billion-dollar corporations. More than a half a dozen institutes of higher learning educate students in a variety of scientific and philosophic disciplines, while voodoo is still practiced openly. Ultra-sophistication and incredible naiveté compete to make south Louisiana unique.

I once met a sociologist from Louisiana State University who told me, "Louisiana politics work like this. A politician tells his constituency, 'I'm going to steal three dollars from you, but I am going to give you one of those dollars back.' As long as the politicians are smart enough to remember the deal, they stay in office. If they forget the deal, they will be voted out. Louisiana has a lot of money; not many of its everyday citizens do, but there is a lot of money to be made in Louisiana—if you can get the go-ahead from the good ol' boys."

Apparently, someone in the Corporation had met the "good ol' boys" and had received the go-ahead to start construction on The Willows Resort. It had begun six months ago in the River Parishes. Isolated, the site had only one road in and out of the area and was surrounded by marsh and wetlands. There was stagnate water, poisonous snakes and voracious mosquitoes to contend with; not to mention alligators.

Gators in a Louisiana swamp are like gators anywhere else, except they are bigger, smarter and meaner. They will lie in wait in the water, floating with just their eyes and nostrils visible. When they strike, it is literally like a lightning bolt.

Gators don't kill their prey by biting as most folks believe. They drown it. Grabbing a victim in his steel-trap jaws, capable of over 2,100 pounds of pressure, the gator begins to roll over and over in the water. Whether the victim is large or small, the gator simply submerges and pulls its struggling victim under. Once drowned, the gator carries its victim's body back to its lair.

This is often just a shallow den or depression in a riverbank or beneath the tangled roots of a toppled tree. Here the gator deposits its victim and allows the body to begin decomposition; which, with the heat and humidity of south Louisiana, does not take very long.

An alligator's teeth are not made for chewing. The gator rips or tears a chunk of meat free. If the victim is small enough, the gator just swallows it whole; otherwise, the body of the prey has to "soften up," or start to rot, to allow pieces to be more easily pulled free. Gators are extremely practical and patient creatures. They have changed little in the past several million years.

Their only real enemy is man. Man has guns, man has boats and man has drained most of their wet marshy swamps. As one Cajun friend of mine is fond of saying, "Ah, de gator, he kills you cause he is hungry and you are supper, but man... man kills 'cause him likes to kill."

Apparently, the Corporation had seen a benefit to locating in south Louisiana. That meant the Corporation wasn't concerned about interference or investigation from the locals, which meant only one thing: someone had been bought and paid for.

That had to be someone special; someone high enough in the state government to spot serious problems that might develop for the Corporation. That person would also have to be in a position to assist in obtaining the land for construction, building permits, etc. That person would have to be influential, corruptible and manageable.

I checked into my hotel before I called a friend of mine, Hugh Clayton, who was a reporter for the *"Times Picayune,"* the New Orleans daily newspaper. Hugh had "immigrated" from north Louisiana fifteen years ago and was still working on being accepted. He was intelligent and well connected. He made a reputation of fair, honest and somewhat politically-centered reporting.

"Hugh Clayton," the voice said, over the telephone connection.

"Hugh, this is 'Doc' Roberts."

"Hey boy," he said, apparently pleased to hear from me. "You still in Houston?"

"Yeah," I answered, "you know me, Texan to the bottom of my boots. I gave you Cajuns the chance to keep me but you screwed it up."

"My foot," he laughed. "You came down here and stole the best looking woman in south Louisiana and then hot-footed it across the border before we could prosecute you."

"I agree. Clay, I met a guy down in Mexico last week," I began. "He was telling us about a new resort called The Willows, somewhere south of Baton Rouge. Have you heard of it?"

"Hell, yes," he said, and I could hear him shuffling papers in the background. "Here it is, The Willows Resort. This thing has never made sense to me."

"What do you mean?" I asked, paying close attention.

"Well, I don't know exactly," he began, "but about a year ago, a lawyer from out west started making inquiries about purchasing some land down here for his client. Not just any land though, he was real specific about the package."

"Well," I asked, "what is so unusual about that? Sounds pretty normal to me."

"I would say you're right until about nine months ago, something new was added." Hugh was telling a story now and nothing I said would hurry him along. "There were several other land proposals in the mill but each had been turned down for one reason or another. Then, along comes the Reverend Henry Mire, he's a fundamental evangelical minister with an offshoot church that has been increasingly active over the last ten years."

"Is that the Glory Word group?" I asked.

"One and the same," Hugh confirmed. "How do you know about it?"

"I just came across it in some research I've been doing. You were saying…"

"Anyway," Hugh continued, "next thing you know, Reverend Mire and this attorney are working together on the project. Within two weeks, a 125-acre section of what had been title-restricted land had been located and purchased. Construction started almost immediately but they didn't use any local construction companies, they all came in from out of state. Everything has been pretty hush-hush. All I know is it sure as hell is not another casino."

"How do you know?"

"Number one, you can't put a casino on public land in Louisiana," he explained. "It has to be on a boat, like in Shreveport or Baton Rouge; or it has to be on Indian land, such as the casinos at Kenner and Marksville. Number two, no publicity. When a casino opens up, everyone knows about it. The casinos begin building a client base a full year before the doors open up. Number three, no local contractors. Casinos always use as many local people as they can; it shows they are buying into the communities. This place was built by outsiders and staffed by outsiders and it is private with a capital 'P'."

"Can you get a list of the principals involved in this project?" I asked, with my fingers crossed.

"Nope, already tried," he responded immediately. "According to all of the court records and titles, the Reverend Henry Mire is the owner. He has declared it a religious retreat and resort and posted all of the land surrounding the construction site. I'll tell you Doc, for a while I was afraid we were going to have another fortress like the one in Waco being built in my backyard."

"Is that still your feeling?"

"To be honest with you, I don't know what to think at this stage. Why are you so interested anyway?" he asked, already smelling at what he thought would be a story.

"Oh hell Hugh, I'm not particularly interested," I lied. "I was simply trying to find a nice place to take Pam for a long weekend."

"Well, scratch that idea," he said, with a laugh. "You couldn't get in that place without an engraved invitation."

"You're probably right," I said, turning the entry pass over and over on the desk. "Thanks for all the info. Give the wife a hug."

"You do the same," he said. "When are we all going back to Grand Isle?"

"I'll have to get back with you on that one." I broke the connection and called John.

Chapter Five

John logged on to several different computer networks; each one presented a different part of the puzzle. Hopscotching across the country and in and out of several different justice agencies resulted in a stack of papers almost an inch thick. It took almost two hours for him to call me back.

"Hello," I said.

"Check your email. I think I've found the info you are looking for," John said. "Call me back after you've had the chance to read what I've sent. I have to run out for a while."

"Roger that." I went to my laptop and printer and powered up. Fifteen minutes later, I had the hard copies in hand and was sorting the loose sheets into appropriate stacks.

Unconsciously, I softly whistled *"The Hall of the Mountain King,"* as I worked. During periods of intense stress or concentration, this song creeps into my memory. Since I was a kid, the song from the *"Pied Piper of Hamlin"* had been special to me. It seemed to focus and settle me for some reason; I've never understood why.

One hour and forty-five minutes later, I sat back, shook my head and dialed John's phone number. It was answered on the first ring.

"That you?" he asked.

"Yeah, you did a good job. What do you think about the good Reverend?"

"Well," John began, "I hate to make a judgment call about someone I have never met, but I think this guy either has had a significant spiritual awakening or he is a con man or worse. Since we have him linked, at least circumstantially, to the Corporation, I lean toward a rather negative view of Reverend Mire. Of course, there may be either legitimate explanations, or the Reverend himself might be one of the victims. However, I can eat a bowl of alphabet soup and shit a better argument than that."

"Have you heard anything from Dave Blaine?" I asked.

"No" John said, "I have a call into him, but he has not returned it yet."

"Okay, my suggestion is we refer the matter of Reverend Mire to the Committee. Let's see what, if anything, they have on the man, his people or the church."

"I'll see what I can do and call you when I have a report," John said, and hung up. He jumped as his phone rang, almost immediately.

"Hello."

"John, this is Dave Blaine. I received your page. How can I help you?"

"I have some information I need to send to you," John said. "It concerns some activities in Louisiana that may be related to our 'friends,' if you follow my meaning."

"Uh-huh, I am sure that I do," Blaine said, after a few seconds. "What do you need from this end?"

"I would appreciate coordination of this information with the Committee. If any information can be added to the picture, it should verify what we believe is another branch of the Corporation."

"Okay, send it to me." Blaine gave him a restricted email address. "I'll run this past the Committee and set up a conference call with you and Doc as soon as I have their report."

"I'll wait for your call," John said. "The information is going out to you as we speak. I'll alert Doc to be on standby. Talk to you soon." John hung up and sent each of the files to Blaine. *It will be interesting*, he thought, *to find out what the Committee comes up with.*

Chapter Six

The Reverend Henry Mire preferred to sound his first name with a silent "H" and the long "e" of the French, as in "On ree." He liked to be called Reverend, it bespoke of his status within the community and his commitment to his flock. HIS flock, he sighed... HIS flock numbered over 1,700 souls; souls HE had rescued from damnation, souls HE had rescued from degradation, souls now committed to serving God through the Reverend Henry Mire.

Sitting at the desk in his office/study, his eyes traveled across the mahogany paneling of the room and the expansive bookcases which ran from floor to ceiling. It was an extensive collection of bound copies of the classics as well as books on psychology, philosophy and religion. He had read none of them.

The Reverend Henry Mire appreciated the complexity of his life as well as its sublime simplicities. He had founded the Church of the Glory Word after a long apprenticeship. He had been a "follower," a necessary trait if one was to aspire to become a "leader."

As a "follower," he had learned the vocabulary and language of salvation. As a "follower," he had learned about sacrifices, subjugation and their rewards. As a "follower," he had followed the instructions of "the Brotherhood."

The Reverend Henry Mire smiled at the thoughts of his successful completion of that apprenticeship. He knew that without the Brotherhood, his life would be very different. Not only would he not be the Reverend Henry Mire, he would not be alive. Therefore, he was committed to the Brotherhood. He was responsible to, and for, the Brotherhood in all that he did.

His "job," Mire smiled at that concept, was to lead the lost and damned out of the pit. His responsibilities included the secular, pastoral counseling of those with troubles and those who had lost their way. As it had been explained to him, he was to "interview the lost," to find those who were capable and worthy of serving. The Brotherhood must be nurtured, cultivated and allowed to grow; he was to facilitate that growth. He was to provide places, people and souls for that nurturing.

Reverend Mire had been successful in his efforts. For fifteen years, the Brotherhood had been nurtured and had been growing. The evidence was all around him; his flock was well on the way to reaching over 2,000 souls.

Of course, as with any religious organization, most of the flock was simply sheep but the mission of sheep is to follow the shepherd. They had followed him well, especially during the last ten years. He relished his success. He liked the home he lived in. He liked the expensive suits his position required of him and provided for him.

Most of all, he liked the adoration of those HE saved. He smiled at the thought of salvation.

Reverend Mire shifted in his seat, and stifled a grin of pleasure as he watched the young girl named Holly. She was good, one of the best workers in the office. She felt her position was a privilege, not just a duty, and certainly not a job. She was devoted to the Reverend Henry Mire.

He had saved her, taking her away from a life that had already killed her older sister and would have killed her. Now, she had the respect of her "family" and the love of the Reverend. She was proud to help him. She was proud of her service to her church. She was finishing her present "assignment" when she noticed the Reverend looking at her.

"Yes, Reverend," she said, smiling and wondering what he was thinking.

"Oh, it's nothing Holly," the Reverend said. "I simply take pleasure in watching you work."

"Thank you, Sir," she smiled again and blushed. "I'm glad you are pleased."

The Reverend Henry Mire stood up, just over six feet tall and still fairly solid for a man in his 50s. She stood up also, pulled a couple of tissues from the box on his desk and wiped her mouth and hands, then shyly left the room. He watched her leave. *She is one of my flock, one that I saved. Merely a child,* he thought, wiping himself off and zipping up his pants before throwing the handful of tissues into the waste can beside his massive, oak desk. *She may be only fifteen, but damn she is good!*

The Reverend was now wealthy, respected and had all of the little boys and girls he could possibly want. He could do things now he could not have dreamed of in the old days. The Brotherhood had rescued him and now it protected him. He protected the Brotherhood and the Brotherhood protected him.

Chapter Seven

Mire thought of his first meeting with a "Brother" fifteen years ago. He was sitting on a bridge that spanned a bayou just outside of Thibodeaux, Louisiana—drunk, destroyed and ready to step off the bridge and into the cold, black water of the bayou. He was ready to die. A black Mercedes had stopped, pulled off the road and a man got out and walked back to him.

"Hello, Father," the man had said.

"Go away, I am not a priest anymore," he said, with a sob. "I have lost my church and my God. I am lost."

The man approached and laid his hand on the former priest's shoulder. "You are not lost my friend. You are simply misunderstood. You are alone in a world whose feelings and desires are vastly different from yours." The man's voice was soft, almost pleading.

He was well dressed, not appearing to take notice of the stench of alcohol that hung like a cloud around the former priest. "Are you interested in seeing a better world, a world in which you not only can exist, but will be valued for who you are?"

"You don't know me!" the former priest cried out. "You don't know what I have done, what I have been doing to these children for years! I am damned and doomed!" Great waves of sobbing racked his body.

The stranger took the former priest by the arm and led him to the black Mercedes. "You are wrong my friend," the stranger said. "I know exactly who you are and exactly what you have done. I have been following your case with interest and have sought you out Father; you specifically. Come with me. Let me introduce you to my friends; stay with us until the end of the week. If you wish at that time, I will bring you back to this bridge and you may end your life without further interruption."

He accepted the proposition and by the end of the week, the former priest had ended his life. It was assumed that the disgraced priest had jumped from that bridge and into the cold, black water of that bayou. His clothes, his billfold and a suicide note were found in a neat bundle next to the guardrail.

But while the priest died, the man who had been the priest simply assumed the mantel of Reverend Henry Mire. He had been, in fact, reborn on that bridge. Reverend Mire had been saved; saved by a man he had not seen before or again since that day. A man named Val Richards.

That was the way the Brotherhood worked. "The Brotherhood finds the lost and gives them light," Reverend Henry Mire said aloud, with a smile. His past became his future; his sins became his virtues. He was now valued for those "eccentricities" that had destroyed his former life.

Established as a respected member of the community, he protected the Brotherhood by contributions to its coffers and by acting as a "visible" proponent for the ideas and projects of the "invisible" fraternity. They, and he, enjoyed a symbiotic relationship. Each contributed something and they had survived very nicely over the past fifteen years.

Chapter Eight

The Baton Rouge City Court is housed in a former school building on Laurel Street. The building's past function was obvious to anyone that approached it. The blackboards and classrooms are gone, replaced by offices and waiting rooms. The students are gone. In their places, criminals, victims, police officers, attorneys and office workers now fill the halls.

I pulled my 1985 Honda Shadow 1100 motorcycle into a parking space at the city court building. I set the kickstand and climbed off the bike. My black chaps, black motorcycle jacket, black gloves, and a black Shoei helmet with a smoked visor, all had a fine coating of dust and road grime.

I had departed Houston that morning at 0600 hours. It was not yet noon. My hands and body still tingled with the vibrations from the bike and the road. My lower back was stiff but the 1100, named Merlin, is a heavy bike that rode easy but it still was a trip of almost 300 miles.

I stretched a couple of times, turned and began walking east toward the Greyhound Bus Station. I pulled off my gloves and slid them under the epaulet on my left shoulder. I undid the chinstrap on the helmet, lifted the visor to remove my glasses and then the helmet.

Instead of going to the bus station, I turned and headed down the grassy slope to the parking lot of a professional medical building. The sign in front read "The DR. J.T. PERRY Building." The building was constructed on stilts with parking spaces below it. In the back corner of the parking area, a man sat on the fender of his car. I moved toward the man and he stood up, his right hand going inside his coat.

"Easy, Mongo," I said, stopping and holding up both hands and the helmet.

"Damn, Junior!" a deep voice boomed, "I didn't know you were coming as Easy Rider." I closed the distance and Mongo removed his right hand. I shook hands with James T. Perry, the son of the man the building was named for.

"Well," he boomed, "you look healthy. How do you feel?"

"I feel good—a little stiff sometimes, but hell I think that is age." I laughed.

Perry smiled. "Hell yeah, it's age. I didn't get shot up and I'm still stiff from the damned 4.5-click run you subjected me too in Mexico."

"Quit bitching," I grinned. "Seems to me you volunteered for that mission. Hell, I remember you making some comment about how your time for that 4.5-click run was a few seconds faster than mine."

"What does that have to do with anything?" Mongo grinned. "You know I have to bitch about something." For almost twenty-three years now, one of Mongo's most consistent traits was that he had to bitch or he would blow up. So far, he hadn't blown up so it must be working.

We had served together on active duty Air Force and over the years had dropped in and out of each other's lives a few times. I looked at my friend and hoped we did not repeat that cycle again. I liked the big man with his deep, bear voice and his big, bear shoulders.

At fifty years old, Mongo, the nickname I had given him better than twenty years ago, was still stronger and meaner than most men half his age. I had seen the big man move; he was fast, he was strong and he was fearless. *If Mongo gets after you, you had better give your soul to the Lord, because your ass belongs to Mongo,* I quoted in my mind.

"I assume the reason you're here is not social," Mongo said, his dark eyebrows bunched in a crease.

"Well, partially social, but you're right, the Corporation has surfaced again." I reached to the inside pocket of my leather jacket and pulled out an envelope, looking around the parking area to be sure we were alone before opening it. I spread the documents out on the hood of Mongo's black Lexus. I explained what information John and Dave Blaine had been able to develop so far. I explained the theory they were operating on, and the fact that at this stage it was total speculation.

"So," Perry began, "I say again, what are you doing here?"

"I'm following up on some Intel leads." I smiled.

"Are we going in?" Perry asked.

"Don't know for sure, but my guess is yes." I pulled a cigar from my jacket and struck a match on the support beam next to Perry's car. Inhaling deeply, I pointed back to the map on the hood. "If this is what it appears to be, we are not going to have any choice. This is the best and first view of the Corporation's stateside business we have. The Committee is anxious to learn more."

"What do you need from me?"

"See what you can find out about this guy." I handed Perry several faxed pages dealing with the Reverend Henry Mire. "He's either the front guy for this operation or he is suckered in way over his head. Don't know which. And see what you can find on the deal for the land The Willows is sitting on. Apparently, Mire had some influence applied in the right places and at the right times to facilitate the deal. I want to know what and who is involved."

"Alright, give me a couple of days." Perry folded the papers back into the envelope. "You staying over?"

"Yeah," I nodded, "I'll be at my son's for the next couple of days. Would you and Mary like to get together for drinks or supper while I'm here?"

"I'd like to, Junior." Perry had given that nickname to me over twenty years ago also. "But let's leave it open and see."

I stuck out my hand. "Take care of yourself."

Mongo stuck out his and we shook. "All the time, Junior." I headed out of the parking area as Perry got into his Lexus.

Ain't life strange? Perry thought. *I didn't think I'd ever see that boy alive again...now here we go again. Ain't life strange?* He adjusted the radio controls, eased the Lexus out of the parking spot and was about to leave the parking area when he stopped to let a pedestrian cross the drive.

I flipped the cigar butt away, took a last look at the Lexus and walked back. Perry gunned the car into traffic and was three miles away by the time I threw my leg over Merlin's seat. "Nice bike," a voice said from behind. I had not turned on the bike's ignition yet and I turned to see a man standing behind me.

"Thanks," I said. "I've had her for a long time."

"What is it, an '87?" The man moved closer.

"An '85," I said, waiting to see where this was going.

"Texas plates I see. You live in Texas?" the man asked.

"Uh-huh," I acknowledged. I buckled on my helmet, slid on my glasses and gloves and started the bike. "Take care, friend," I said, and drove away. Once I was in traffic, I watched my rear view mirror. Sure enough, a yellow Monte Carlo pulled out; in it, I counted three heads.

Crossing the railroad tracks and driving past the Flowers Bakery Company of Baton Rouge, I pulled into the right-hand lane and set the cruise control lever on Merlin's throttle. The Monte Carlo was pacing me from the left lane.

I know what they're thinking, I thought. *An old man on a classic bike and he is from Texas. He has on new riding leathers and a three hundred dollar helmet. Three against one and no one around here will even be looking for him. Easy pickings.* "NOT!"

I headed out on Florida Boulevard toward Denham Springs, a small town east of Baton Rouge. Six years ago, I had lived in Baton Rouge and remembered a section of road between the two towns that was un-populated. It crossed the Amite River; on this side, a dirt road ran down to the riverbank. A good place to fish in the spring and summer, not many people would be around this time of the year. I turned left on State Highway 426 and turned right and headed toward the S & S Lounge.

Fifty feet past the lounge, I turned left and drove off the road and shifting into third slowed; the Monte Carlo continued to pace my progress on the bike. Leaving the black top road, I slowed Merlin way down on the dirt and gravel. An 1100 is not a dirt bike, so I had to use my legs and periodically stand on the foot pegs to take the shock of the nearly non-existent road to help control the bike.

In the mirror I saw the Monte Carlo was still following at a distance. Pulling behind a dirt mound, covered in three-foot tall vegetation, I turned Merlin around, now facing the way I had come and killed the engine. I saw the dust cloud of an approaching vehicle over the brush and cane.

I took off my helmet, set it on the handlebars and walked away from the bike. Still stiff from the long ride, I stretched and did a couple of toe touches and knee bends to loosen up. *I am really getting too old for this shit,* I thought.

The Monte Carlo pulled up, stopping about thirty feet from Merlin. Three people got out; one was the man I talked to in the parking lot. He was black, 6 foot, about 150 pounds with a goatee on his chin. He had not shaved the rest of his face for several days; the effect was comical. It looked like textured carpet.

Next was a white guy, about 5 foot, 10 inches tall and 180 pounds with the worst case of acne I had ever seen. Red splotches replaced what would have been a complexion; several of the pimples were in-fected and pus was running from one on his neck.

He looked about eighteen and appeared mean instead of tough—cunning instead of smart.

Last was a woman, well actually a girl; well, actually a bitch. At about 5 feet, 5 inches tall, she couldn't weigh more than 100 pounds. She carried a pistol and her eyes were wild; it was obvious she was on something, meth or crack cocaine, both which are drugs of choice in this area.

"Friends," I called from the shadows, "I get the feeling you have an interest in me. I'm just an old man out for a ride." My voice came from nowhere and yet from everywhere; the three froze. I had chosen this spot with care; I knew they couldn't see me.

"Young lady," I said, as I watched them trying to decide where I was, "I would appreciate if you would drop that pistol. Fellas, why don't you take the lady out of here and we can all live to see the sunset."

For a minute, I thought they might actually listen to reason but that minute passed and the three separated and started moving apart. A blue heron started to fly over but swerved and landed closer to the river; he knew something bad was about to happen. Clouds of yellow dirt that had puffed with their footsteps settled on their shoes.

I could taste the salt of the sweat that ran down my cheek and settled in the crook of my lips, and smelled the aroma and dampness of the river vegetation along its bank. I felt the rubber grips of the special .45 caliber pistol I carry when I ride Merlin.

A stainless steel Model 1911 frame, the slide and frame had been shortened until it looked like an Officer's Model but with eight shots instead of six. I had nicknamed the gun "Joe" after Vinegar Joe Stillwell, an old Army General.

"Kids, this is your last chance. Let's go home, please." The girl fired at the sound of my voice, she missed—I didn't. The bullet caught her at the bridge of her nose directly between her eyes. Her body was snapped back, head first. I stepped out of the shadows and quietly ordered, "Freeze."

The two men froze, then went for the guns they had under their shirts. They didn't make it. I fired twice at each man. My first shot caught the white man once in the gut. The second round smashed squarely in his erupting, acne-flushed face. The black man took one high in the right shoulder and flipped. The second shot missed.

I walked over to the black man and stepped on his gun, hand pinning a Smith .38 snub nose to the ground. He looked up and with a mixture of fear, anger and pain, whispering, "You son of a bitch. I ain't going back to jail. I just got out when I spotted you and I ain't goin' back."

"You know, for probably the first time in your sorry life, you're absolutely correct," I said, with neither humor nor mercy. The gunshot was not heard by the afternoon traffic on the bridge a half-mile away. I rammed home a fresh 8-round magazine and hunted around for the six expended .45 caliber cartridges I had fired. I put them in my jacket pocket, cranked Merlin up and drove slowly back to the road.

I went on to Denham Springs, got on Interstate-12 and returned to Baton Rouge from a totally different direction. Every few miles, I pulled a spent cartridge from my pocket. Using my gloves to smear the surface of each cartridge to obliterate any prints, I flipped each cartridge toward the shoulder of the road. By the time I arrived at my son's house, all of the cartridges were gone.

I had packed an extra barrel and an extra slide for Joe; when I changed them out, nothing could tie the gun to the shootings. I would simply retire the suspect barrel to target shooting. After several hundred rounds, the ballistic patterns would be altered.

The old slide would require a new extractor and re-facing the area adjacent to the firing pin before it could be used again. This would keep it from being linked to any shells that might be found. There was less than a million to one chance any would ever be found; but if one did surface, neither the cartridge nor a slug from one of the bodies would ever be linked to Joe or to me.

I'd leave the old slide and barrel in my son's shop. It might not be a good idea to have them found in my possession on the return trip; I would retrieve them later. I made a mental note to call Dave Blaine tomorrow and explain what had happened and why, but there were things I had to take care of today.

Chapter Nine

When I pulled into the driveway, my granddaughter, Her Highness Sarah the First, was driving her battery-powered Jeep around and around in the backyard. I revved Merlin's engine and then turned off the bike and set the kickstand. Sarah squealed and hollered, "PawPaw." She jumped from the Jeep and ran toward me. I scooped her up and got a big hug and kiss.

"Hey, Bonehead," I said. It was my current nickname for her and the second in what I hoped would be a long line of silly names that would continue over the upcoming years.

"Hey, PawPaw," she said, "I missed you. Where's PamMaw?"

"She could not come this time, baby, but she sent you a big kiss and here it is." I smacked her very loudly on the cheek. Innocence was a beautiful thing after the episode I had just left. Her dad, my son, stepped out of the garage.

"Hey, Old Man," he said, as we hugged. He stopped suddenly and pushed back from the embrace. "Problems?"

"Three," I said. "I'm okay, they're not."

John looked past my shoulders at the traffic. "No one is coming."

"It got settled about forty-five minutes ago and I did several round-abouts before I came here," I said.

"You sure you're okay?"

"Body, yes. Spirit? Speaking of spirits, I'd love a drink; got any Jack?" I asked, and started walking to the house. Once inside, I phoned Pam while John poured us both a drink. I left a message that I had arrived safely and would call her later this evening. John brought the drinks and we sat outside watching Her Highness drive her Jeep. I briefed John on what had happened and what I planned to do about it.

"Sounds like you have all of the bases covered," John said.

I smiled. "Think so, in any event, what's done is done." I steered the discussion toward Reverend Henry Mire. John had become more familiar with the Church of the Glory Word, one of a multitude of evangelistic "religious" orders that had popped up in the south; the Church of the Glory Word was one of the more active.

He said, "I first started hearing about Mire and the so-called church a few years ago. It seems to have doctrine and rituals that mingle both Catholic and Protestant ideas, the church has a mixed but loyal following. They recently started doing a televangelist show; it's a big hit."

"He has the personality for that?" I asked.

"Mire is articulate and obviously well versed in religious doctrine and procedures and not one to shun publicity; in fact, he embraces it," John explained. "However, little was known of Reverend Mire before his appearance fifteen years ago. He says, 'I have come from far away and through many changes to stand here before you today.' He's had a significant impact on the lost and homeless masses in several large south Louisiana cities. He has a real appeal to the lower and middle-income white male population; and, those who feel disenfranchised by the actions of government and society.

"Even though the focus of Mire's ministry is on the poorer of society, his church appears to be solvent; even flourishing. They're based in Baton Rouge for the past three years and just purchased and converted a large furniture store on Airline Highway. The remodeling took almost four months to complete, but apparently the result has been worth the wait. The Cathedral, as it is called, supposedly is magnificent; a place worthy of being televised, which was his plan all along."

John explained that Louisiana's televangelist community has had significant ups and downs over the last several years. Scandal and slander rocked the foundations of the evangelical community but Mire appeared to prosper. So far no dirt had attached itself to the Reverend's heavenly robes although, three years before, there had been a man who claimed to know Reverend Mire.

The man had claimed to "know who the Reverend was and what he had done." After hinting at accusations directed to the Reverend, strangely, the man had been killed the next day in a one-car vehicle accident near Gonzales, just south of Baton Rouge.

The story was that his car left the road and landed in a bayou near French Settlement at 10:00 P.M. It was 7:30 the next morning before anyone spotted the car and an hour later before the vehicle, a 1986 Oldsmobile, was removed from the bayou and the body recovered.

Drug paraphernalia in the car, old and new tracks on his right arm, plus significant levels of cocaine in his blood, and a blood alcohol content of .133, were sufficient to close the case as "accidental death due to drug impairment." The man was forgotten and his claims were never made public.

*****

As an Air Force cop, I began studying the phenomenon of serial offenders, serial rapists and pedophiles over ten years ago; more of a hobby than anything. Luckily, I was able to use that research as I prepared a paper for my Master's in Police Science. While I can intellectually accept the reality of those individuals, I cannot emotionally.

The FBI Behavioral Science Unit, still called the BS Unit by friends and foes alike, had coined the term sexual psychopath. Sex for these people took a perverted twist somewhere along the way. A sexual psychopath can be a serial rapist, a pedophile or both. If the victims habitually die, the appropriate term becomes serial killer.

While it's true that serial killers are predominantly men, women do murder but their murders are historically incidental. Women seldom "hunt"; they murder out of rage, out of fear, out of desperation. While they do kill, women predominately kill people who are emotionally close to them, and these killings are more reactive in nature.

For example, Karla Faye Tucker was the first woman executed in Texas since the Civil War. She was a killer who brutally murdered two victims with a pickaxe, leaving the implement buried in the chest of one of her victims. One of many female death row inmates, Tucker made national and international news. During her stay in prison, she claimed to have "found God." The national and international media poured into Texas demanding clemency for Tucker.

Whether or not her conversion was real, only she and God would ever know. Religious convergence or not, she committed a brutal, double murder. She had been legally sentenced to death. If, in those ensuing years she truly found peace with her Maker, that's marvelous. Her victims did not have that time to prepare; their families did not have time to say good-bye.

While the number of female killers has increased, female predators remain, even today, uncommon. The male remains the primary killer of the Homo sapien species, the primary abuser of the species. However, man can overcome the male; being male is an accident of birth—being a man is a choice of conscience.

Males make up the predominance of sexual psychopaths, even though females make their appearance, the male dominates the scene. Sexual deviance, behavior considered outside society's norm but which consenting adults engage in, remains a private matter; but sexual deviance in which one party is an unwilling participant, is a criminal act.

Sex has little to do with pleasure for the sexual psychopath; they seduce and rape to establish control, to dominate, to manipulate. They trick, humiliate and degrade their victims. Now, it seemed the perversion had moved to the corporate level with an organization dedicated to perversion.

A business that services a world where the abnormal was normal, protecting its clients and allowing... No, encouraging them to give vent to their darkest dreams. A world where the despicable was considered divine. It was a world that had victims instead of lovers; a world the TAC Team was committed to destroy.

Chapter Ten

Three days later, we had made a loose recon of the area The Willows Resort was in, studied maps, and aerial photos of the area. Headed back to Houston, I was cruising over the Mississippi River Bridge headed west on Interstate-10. Merlin was running well, the weather was comfortable and the traffic was not bad. I had it timed to arrive back home a little before Pam came home from work.

I wanted to get a shower and relax for a few minutes since I knew it was going to be a late night catching her up on what had happened and what I had learned. I set the cruise control and listened to "my" music. I had installed a cassette player in my left saddlebag and mounted a speaker in my helmet.

I enjoyed listening to Tom Jones. One of his best albums included, of all things, "*Ghost Riders in the Sky*" and along with other western songs it featured one of my favorites, "*Two Brothers.*"

On a sunny day, on a big bike, Tom and I sang out mightily, "One wore blue and one wore gray, as they went along their way. A fife and drum began to play, allllll on a beautiful morning."

It brought back good memories of a long time ago, other lives and other times. At Lake Charles, Louisiana, I topped off the fuel tank, grabbed a soft drink and was back on the road.

A little after noon, I pulled into the driveway, got the mail out of the box and called Pam's office and left a message on her voicemail. I checked my voicemail and email; found some messages, including one from Mongo and one from John. I decided to wait to read them until I had showered.

I rolled Merlin into the garage, stowed the bike gear, stripped and took a scalding shower. The hot water refreshed me and loosened up the muscles from the five-hour ride.

Clean clothes and my moccasins, I felt like a new man. I fed the dogs and the fish, poured a drink and went to the computer; by this time, I had a message from Dave Blaine. There was a wealth of information relating to Reverend Henry Mire and The Willows Resort.

John and David had been able to access and cross check phone records and other data relating to Mire's activities. John had also discovered that many of his calls were made to phone numbers we had obtained during the Mexico mission. Circumstantial?

Sure, but I don't believe in coincidence. In police work, if it looks like a duck, quacks like a duck and runs with other ducks, it's a damned duck. You just have to PROVE it to the satisfaction of the legal system— sometimes easier said than done.

I was setting up a conference call with John and Dave when the universe played one of its wild cards. As I dialed Dave's number, the call-waiting signal interrupted and I decided to take the call.

"Dad?" It was John; I heard something in his voice.

"Yeah, what's the matter?"

"Mongo's been hurt."

"Where is he and how bad is it?" I asked, ready for the worst.

"We don't know how bad it is yet. I'm headed to the Baton Rouge General Hospital. I got the call and identification over my police radio."

"Do you know what happened?" I asked.

"A damned drunk driver, at THIS time of the damned day!" His concern now mixed with anger.

"I'm on my way. I'll meet you at the General." I hung up the phone and started out the door when I remembered I was supposed to call Dave. I called Pam, she answered. I told her what I knew and asked her to call Dave. I promised to call when I had something to report. It was the longest drive of my life, not knowing what I would find when I got to Baton Rouge.

*****

It rained from Lake Charles to Baton Rouge; that heavy, relentless, nasty rain which only comes in Louisiana. The kind that keeps a half step ahead of the windshield wiper on its fastest setting, but just this side of forcing you to pull over and wait until it stops. The wind blew like hell and it was cold, a wet cold soaked through my boots and jacket, even the walls of my pickup. I was glad to be in my pickup instead of on Merlin.

Crossing the Mississippi River Bridge, I barely saw the top of the capital building obscured in a dark cloud that seemed to sit on the city; it was as black as my mood.

I drove straight to the General, one of Baton Rouge's finest hospitals. I knew their standard of medical care was outstanding. *It had better be*, I thought gravely. I parked my truck, pulled on my hat and stepped into the downpour. My slicker and wide-brimmed hat went even blacker; my steps slow and measured. I was in no hurry to find out how bad it was, but I couldn't avoid it either.

Entering the emergency room area, I saw John dressed in the black duty uniform of the LSU Police Department. Louisiana State University functions as a municipality and its officers carry a full state commission, unlike the old campus security forces I was familiar with. LSU Police Department boasts a motorcycle division and its own special weapons and tactics squad called Special Tactics and Response Team, commonly referred to as START.

As any small police force does, it has its problem children, a couple of which are real assholes. But it also boasts several outstanding police officers; one of them my son, he was on both teams.

He saw me and came toward me with his head turned as he talked into his shoulder microphone. His eyes were grave and he was not smiling. I knew it was bad, just not how bad. He finished speaking and grasped my hand, hard. "It isn't looking good, Pop," he said, softly.

John had known Mongo since he and I had been on active duty with the Air Force; John was eight at the time. He continued, "Damned drunk driver left his house to get more beer, ran a stop sign and smashed into him as he crossed the street. He never had a chance."

"How bad?" I asked, not trusting my voice any further.

"Both arms and both legs broken, internal injuries, we don't know how bad yet." He stopped and looked me squarely in the eyes, "He's still unconscious. They say his brain was traumatized and is swollen."

"Prognosis?"

"We, they—the doctors—just don't know," he said, without much hope.

Chapter Eleven

Reverend Mire answered the phone on his polished desktop with a flourish, "Good day and God bless. This is Reverend Mire, may I help you?" The voice on the other end froze his attention.

"Good morning Reverend, this is Kim." Mire recognized the voice immediately as Kim Rhodes.

"Yes Kim, how can I help you?" Mire asked, with hesitation.

"Oh, but Reverend, it is I that can help you." The voice was a mixture of culture and aloofness, of politeness and contempt. "It has come to my attention that *you* have come to the attention of some others."

"Kim, I'm sorry, but I have no idea what you are talking about!" Mire was seriously concerned. A call from Kim Rhodes always meant trouble.

"That is what concerns me, Henry!" Kim's voice now dripped with anger. That "reverend" had been dropped, and the English pronunciation of Henry was used instead of "On-ree," told Mire it was not going to be a good day.

"It appears that several inquiries have been made concerning you and The Willows Resort in the last few days. Why have I not heard from you on these matters?" The voice was like iron ringing on iron.

"Kim, this is the first I have heard about it. Seriously, I have no idea what you are talking about. You know I would have called immediately with any information on a situation like this." Mire was serious and on the verge of tears.

"Now, now Reverend," Kim's voice almost purring. "Perhaps I misspoke. Obviously, you had no knowledge of the inquiries. I can understand that since my security parameters far exceed yours. I'll tell you what, check things out and call me with a report."

"Yes Kim, yes I will. Give me just a little time to research it." Mire was sweating.

"Certainly, my dear Reverend," the purring changed in mid stride and the iron flashed back just before Kim Rhodes slammed the phone in Reverend Henry Mire's ear. "You have one fucking hour."

Kim Rhodes smiled an enigmatic smile; almost everything he did was that way, enigmatic. Kim toyed with the metal paperweight on his desk, the Chinese symbol yin-yang. It was supposed to denote balance in the world and in all human endeavors.

It is a round circle divided into two tear-shaped halves—one black, one white. Within each was a single circle comprised of the other color. Within the black was a pearl of pure white, within the white was a drop of darkness. Kim balanced the symbol on its edge and spun it with a polished and well-manicured fingernail.

Kim took the symbol very personally. Nothing Kim ever encountered had as much meaning as this symbol or spoke so clearly to the heart and soul of Kim Rhodes. It was as though God had spoken directly to Kim with a message everything was, in fact, normal and that Kim Rhodes was, in fact, part of God's overall scheme—if one believed in God, which Kim did not.

Chapter Twelve

Had he believed in God, Kim Rhodes would have hated Him; supposedly all powerful, incapable of making mistakes. He had made one mistake. Kim Rhodes would have professed anger at God's incompetence. Kim Rhodes' life had been a mistake. Kim Rhodes was not his birth name.

Born to a lower middle class family, Kim Rhodes was now exceedingly rich. Born and raised to be an item of ridicule, Kim Rhodes was now to be envied. Born to spend life in poverty, Kim Rhodes walked the pavilions of the wealthy. Born to live in fear, Kim Rhodes now created fear in others. Born and made to wish for death, death was now what he enjoyed providing. Kim Rhodes killed people for a living.

In most circumstances, Kim Rhodes could have been called a hitman, but that would not have been exactly correct. In other circumstances, Kim could have been called a hit woman, but that would not have been exactly correct either; nor was the term hit person exactly correct.

Kim Rhodes was all and none of these. Kim was simply a force, neither male nor female and yet both; a hermaphrodite, a person with the genitalia of both sexes. Kim had developed many skills during a lifetime that only spanned thirty-three years—the first of which had been survival.

He was not a normal baby. The midwife who delivered him had not seen the problem; his mother's complications had caused the midwife to focus on her. Luckily, or unluckily, his mother survived. She was only a child herself and it was days after the birth before she discovered that John had both a penis and a vagina.

Hermaphrodites are not as uncommon as people think but when the condition is discovered, it usually is surgically corrected. Rarely is it talked about and unless problems surface years later, it becomes a non-issue. In most cases, hormonal therapy and supplementation will stabilize and correct the confusion that results from the non-specific, sexual determination at birth. There had been no attempts made to correct the baby's problem.

His fourteen-year-old mother had no money of her own and his father, in fact his own grandfather, would do nothing that would expose the issue. His mother was simply "a troubled girl who had gotten in trouble with the boys."

His mother had been the subject of her father's attention for several years and he became the result of that attention. To his father/grandfather, John was simply the result of his own daughter's stupidity. The grandfather never accepted responsibility for the child or the issues related to either his misbehavior with his daughter or the resulting birth of his son/grandson.

As he grew older, he began to find himself the subject of his grandfather's attention—as a victim. One day, at thirteen years of age, after being the old man's toy for several years, Kim had walked into the old man's study and calmly blew the old bastard's head off with a 12-gauge, double-barrel shotgun.

Kim carefully staged the scene, having planned the "accident" for months. Law enforcement officials in the area were only too happy to accept the explanation and the evidence that the old man had died as a result of an accidental gunshot while cleaning his weapon.

The insurance money came, the will was probated and the estate was settled. Kim was now the only son of a very rich, young woman. He had his first kill and he had gotten away with it; his second kill would not come about for two years. His mother married shortly after her father was buried.

Kim's new stepfather was a local boy with big dreams, no money of his own, a bad drinking problem and a worse temper. The second time he beat Kim, the boy made up his mind that enough was enough. He figured out how to leak gas into the basement below the study where his stepfather liked to sit at the big desk and drink fine whiskey while smoking a good cigar. When the explosion occurred, several things happened almost at once.

His stepfather was incinerated, his mother died as a result of the heavy door from the study slamming into her at almost sixty miles an hour, and all records of his birth were destroyed by the resulting fire; as was all evidence of his crime. His mother's death had been an accident, which was all right with him; his birth had been an accident.

Kim demonstrated his intelligence and was declared an emancipated adult. With money from his own trust fund, he hired a lawyer from Mobile, Alabama. Even with a healthy chunk of the funds going to the attorney, he remained a wealthy, young man. He put himself into a prep school in New England and survived learning how to be another person.

He had never been comfortable with his own identity anyway. He never worried about who he was, just what he was. During the next four years, he had the opportunity to experiment and try on new aspects of his developing persona and his troubled sexuality. It was a time of discovery.

During one of these episodes, he discovered he liked to kill and from that moment on, he constructed a new person. A person to be feared and a person he would become when he had all of the training necessary for success. During another episode, he discovered that as ambiguous as his body was, so was his interest in sex. He felt attraction to either and both sexes and was well equipped to explore those attractions.

During one escape, he discovered Val Richards at an elegant but exclusive night spot on the east side of Hartford, Connecticut. Kim went for an evening of quiet, sophisticated relaxation but that was the night his life changed forever.

It was the night a blond-headed man came up to his table, seated himself without permission and introduced himself, "Hello, I am Val Richards, mind if I join you?" Life was never the same again.

Chapter Thirteen

The hours crept by and turned into days; Mongo's condition had not changed. Physically he was making progress, but something had happened when his head slammed into the road surface. Finally, the doctor said, "He's still in a coma. He may wake up in ten minutes, ten days, ten years or never. We don't know."

As I drove back to my son's house, memories filled my mind, tears filled my eyes and dread filled my heart. I did not want to lose Mongo but I did not want him to have to live like this.

Then selfishly, I recognized part of my problem was we—the TAC Team—were headed back in harm's way and I did not feel comfortable without Mongo onboard. The next morning I headed back to Houston; Mongo would be out this time and that left a hole in my comfort zone about nine miles across.

I called Pam to let her know I made it back home safely. I unlocked my foot locker and pulled out the dossiers I had put together when I picked the team that had confronted the evil known as Val Richards.

During that last mission, and even afterwards, I had searched diligently for Mike Staten, the one I called the Dago. Once, I even thought I had found him, but I was wrong.

Now circumstances dictated I try to redouble my search efforts in earnest now; I needed to fill some gaps. There were three candidates I really wanted. Two of the guys had been on my original TAC Team at Blytheville Air Force Base: George Champlain and Steve English.

Another had been my partner at Clark Air Base, his name was John Morris. John was a tall, slender black man who held several black belts and had distinguished himself in Vietnam. I struck out on all of them, too much time had passed; maybe one day I'd find them. Maybe.

I moved on to Lou Davis, he and I had been on-again-off-again friends for over ten years. He was an ex-Army, Vietnam LRRP, pronounced "Lurp," it stands for Long Range Reconnaissance Patrol. The LLRPs were small, heavily armed teams that patrolled deep in enemy-held territory during the Vietnam War.

The concept dated back to the origins of warfare itself; however, in modern times, these specialized units evolved from examples such as the Long Range Desert Group and the British SAS or Special Air Service Teams during the Second World War.

By 1967, formal LRRP companies were organized, most having three platoons, each with five six-man teams equipped with VHF/FM AN/PRC-25 radios. LRRP training was notoriously rigorous and team leaders were often graduates of the U.S. Army's 5th Special Forces Recondo School in Nha Trang, Vietnam.

There were no satellite communications then, those were a thing of the future. The best available was radio communications for Intel. LRRP Teams had extraordinary kill ratios, sometimes reported as high as 400 enemy troops for every LRRP killed.

Davis had returned home and was treated like the rest of the returning Nam vets—with disrespect and hatred. I had lost track of Lou; the last time I saw him was at a Mardi Gras parade in south Louisiana. I found him outside of Austin, Texas. Quiet, reserved, almost withdrawn sometimes, Lou carried the phantoms and ghosts back from the jungles with him.

Nowadays, they were calling it PTSD, Post Traumatic Stress Disorder; he managed it better than many of the Nam veterans but still carried scars on his soul.

Louis A. Davis, Call Sign: Yankee Clipper
Age: 49
Current Location: Central TX
Physicals   White, Male 6', Brown/Hazel

Military: LRRP, Long Range Reconnaissance Patrol, Army, Vietnam.

Background: Born to a Navy family growing up was an every four year move until he reached NASB, Maine. He graduated from high school in 1966. Attended the University of Maine, Southwestern University. After short periods with the United States Army and Portland Police Dept., Portland, ME, went into the family business in healthcare administration. Owned and operated hospitals and nursing homes for twenty-one years.

Proficient in wood working and construction. Likes most sports, such as Golf, hunting (for food), fishing (for food), Alpine Skiing, water skiing, SCUBA diving although no longer certified, proficient. He is a more than competent boat skipper.

Weapons: Proficient small bore indoor match rifles. Shot indoor match for the US Army, Military .308 sniper, M-14 starlight and sniper equipped, expert qualified M-16 and Browning .45 cal military issue as well as a Smith & Wesson .38 and .357 police issue wheel guns. Personal weapons choice in a long gun is a .35 Cal Marlin lever action. Close quarters in an M-1 carbine. Personal choice in hand guns includes a 9mm Belgian WWII issue, as well as a .380 Llama hide-out gun. As an accomplished bird hunter shotguns are second nature. Personals include but not limited to Win 97 pump, Win 1400 (12's), Savage 20-gauge and a Savage short barrel 410 single shot. Also an avid archer, compound class and cross bow hunter.

STATUS: ACTIVE (Assignment – open)

Chapter Fourteen

My next call was to Zach Stone in Tennessee. I'd known Zach since 1979 and even had a couple of business opportunities with him; he is a... most unusual man. Looking like a cross between the actor Michael J. Fox and a Munchkin, he has an erudite business mind and an insatiable sense of right and wrong.

Standing only five feet, five inches in height, he is perfect for the role of a Monkey Man on the TAC Team; small enough to get in and out of tight spaces the rest of us could not and was a good shot and a tactical thinker. After a hitch in the Army during the Vietnam era as a Cobra Attack Helicopter pilot, he pulled the plug and went into business.

Rated as a "problem solver," he had made his reputation as a magician; turning businesses around from failure to profit centers with his "out of the box" approach. Other advantages? He had maintained his physical fitness at a higher level than the average person in his financial and age bracket and he liked fast cars and well-made firearms.

"Hey Zach," I said, when he answered. "Have you got a minute?" Thirty minutes later, we were set for a face-to-face sit down in Little Rock, Arkansas in two days.

Then I called Marcus Caine, a twenty-three-year-old Army troop who had been medically discharged when he injured his back after Operation Desert Shield. He was good kid and a solid shooter; his only real problem was a lack of direction as to what to do with himself after getting hurt.

Mark and I had met at the American Legion and connected. At a local sports bar over drinks, I eased into the subject. After an hour I said, "So, there it is... I'm two men short and I think you could be one of them."

He didn't hesitate. "Man, this sounds like exactly what I need, Doc. I'm going nuts; finished my rehab, the back is solid. I just can't find anyone willing to give me a job."

"Don't do this for the money, Mark. There is a real element of danger, you need to understand that."

He nodded, "Yeah, I get it. What about equipment?"

"Bring your own. We don't have time to retrain you new guys to a standard weapon. I want you to carry what you're familiar with and willing to hang your life on. Let me know what you want and I'll have all of the practice and mission ammo you need."

"What's my call sign; can I pick my own?"

"Negative, already have it. You're going to be PIMA."

"Puma, I like that."

"No dumbass; PIMA, with an I."

"PIMA, what the hell does it stand for?"

"Pain in my ass," I said, with a smile.

He grinned, "I damn sure am that, aren't I?" He bought the next round of drinks.

Marcus Caine, Call Sign: PIMA
Age: 23
Current Location: Houston, TX
Physicals: White, Male, Brown/Blue

Military: Army, Desert Storm
Weapons: AR-15, Mossberg 870 12-gauge shotgun with a flip up rear stock. He carries and an over-the-shoulder rig, .45 Colt Model 1911 Pistol, and anything else he can get his hands on.

<u>Strengths:</u> Advanced Infantry Tactics

STATUS: ACTIVE (Assignment - open)

Chapter Fifteen

The drive from Houston to Little Rock took a solid seven hours; I had missed the morning rush hour and traffic on Highway 59 and Interstate-30 was moderate. The weather had been clear but the heat of the day had not dissipated yet.

Following Zach's directions, I parked and walked about 150 yards to a secluded overlook of the Arkansas River. The Arkansas River flows southward from the central portion of the state, through the rich delta farmlands before it meets up with the Mississippi. We were two miles downstream from Big Rock, a 200-foot bluff located on the north bank.

This smaller outcropping was known as the Little Rock; from it the capital city of Arkansas got its name. I found Zach sitting on the Little Rock. "So, this is the real Little Rock," I said, wiping the sheen of sweat from my face as I sat down next to him. "I never knew where the name Little Rock came from."

Zach nodded, "This is it. The first European to record the bluffs was French explorer Jean-Baptiste Bénard de La Harpe back in 1722. He called Big Rock 'Le Rocher Français' meaning the French Rock. Here at the 'Petit Rocher' or Little Rock, it was possible to ford the river and a settlement developed. Big Rock wasn't settled much because the north bank was lower and tended to flood. So tell me more about what you mentioned the other day."

Over the next hour and a half, I talked and Zach listened; occasionally taking notes. With a handshake, I closed the deal.

Zach Stone, Call Sign: Mighty Mouse

Age: 48

Current Location: Tennessee

Physicals: White, Male 5'5" Brown/Blue

<u>Military</u>: Warrant Officer, Army, Vietnam

<u>Background</u>: Born In Tennessee. Attended University of Tennessee.

Owned and operated an athletic store and health club for 15 years. Real estate and business development continues after 15 years. Proficient in residential and commercial construction. Enjoys motorsports. Participates in SCCA (Sports Car Club of America) racing events.

<u>Weapons</u>: Proficient AH-1 Cobra Attack Helicopter. Snub Smith Model 60, Browning Hi Power 9mm, Mini-14 and a Ruger Mark 2 with internal silencer, .22 caliber.

<u>Strengths</u>: Problem solving and tactical Helo Ops

STATUS: ACTIVE (Assignment - open)

Chapter Sixteen

When I got back to Houston the next evening, I found a strange phone message from another friend, John Battaglia. John and I had worked together on several civilian projects, his mind constantly shifted from topic to topic at lightning speed. Personally I had always felt he had ADD, Attention Deficit Disorder, but when he focused he was damn good. John had never served in the military but had been a private fixed-wing pilot for a number of years.

As I listened, a thought hit me; I could use a pilot for this operation to transport items that required some "sensitive handling." I called him back and pitched the idea; he jumped on it.

John is a big man, with a dark complexion, a heavy mustache and an Italian ancestry. He came up with his own call sign, Godfather. The numbers were beginning to add up in my favor, finally.

John N. Battaglia, Call Sign: Godfather
Age: 48
Current location: Central, Colorado

Physicals: White, Male, 5'11", Brown/Brown
Background: Born and educated in New Jersey, Battaglia graduated high school in 1969. He attended college finally getting a degree in Engineering. Possesses a high degree of mechanical ability, highly involved in automobile construction, modification and restoration. He enjoys metal work and is proficient in general construction.

He is a licensed and active private pilot checked out in: Cessna 150, Cessna 152, and the Cessna 172 Piper Cherokee, Piper Arrow II complex. He prefers single engine land aircraft and is competent in cross-country navigation and night flying.

Weapons: Primary handguns include a .40 Glock and a 9mm Ruger. Proficient with .22 Ruger Mark II, a Beretta .25 and a .38 wheel gun. Primary long guns include a scoped Yugoslavian SKS modified to accept the 30-round magazine and a 9mm High Point carbine he nicknamed "the Little Nasty" for close work. Carries a Glock Combat Knife with a WWII Trench Knife as back up. With a strong background in chemistry, he is self-taught in pyrotechnics.

STATUS: ACTIVE (Logistics and fixed wing pilot)

*****

Going through dossiers was what Dan Briggs and Jim Phelps had made famous on the old TV series "*Mission Impossible*." It was what I had done repeatedly for the Air Force and with the original TAC Team. The difference was... this wasn't a TV show; it was reality, a deadly reality.

Chapter Seventeen

Kim Rhodes once described Val Richards as "sophisticated, urbane and insatiable, both in bed and out of bed. His moods were mercurial, his tendency toward excess was unbelievable. Yet, his mind worked like a fine watch, always a step ahead of anyone around him."

For someone like Rhodes, it was incredible to see someone with so much passion, so much determination and someone so absolutely sure of himself. Kim began to study Val Richards and Val enjoyed the naiveté of Kim Rhodes. He viewed Kim as an empty canvas, unmolded clay that could become anything he wanted him to become.

For Kim, there was the excitement of discovering he could become anything, or anyone, he wanted to be. For Val, there was the excitement of creating anything, or anyone, he wanted. Neither would say they *loved* the other.

Both simply recognized a need the other could supply. Both knew when Val Richards sat down that night, the person who Kim Rhodes had been began to die, and a new person was being born.

Discarding his birth name, Val picked the name Kim, because it was a name that identified an individual, not a male individual or a female individual, just an individual. Since Kim was neither male nor female, but both, what better choice for his new name than a name that was neither and both male and female.

Val had given him the yin-yang paperweight and told him, "This reminds me of you, being neither aspect of normal, you create a newness that is only you." Val had even incorporated the symbol when he designed the logo for the Corporation. Upon graduation from prep school, one person passed into oblivion and Kim Rhodes stepped out of the mist.

Val knew about and approved of Kim's predilection for killing. They had discussed it several times over the preceding two years. Val placed Kim in training with the finest martial arts instructors he could find and Kim took to the training like a natural. He learned to shoot firearms from the best, learned archery from the best, learned explosives from the best.

It fascinated Val that sometimes Kim would appear as a male student, sometimes as a female student. Slender, with refined features, Kim was equally believable in both personas. For Val, it was literally like having two lovers, one male and one female and having the perfect employee. When a problem presented itself that required a "final solution," Kim became that solution.

Kim killed with precision and intelligence; nothing was wasted, nothing was flamboyant... nothing excessive. Each "accident" he created was utterly believable. So when a message had to be given, Kim delivered in a way that there was no question as to what the message was, or from whom it came.

There was absolutely no discernible pattern to the killings—no two were similar. Had they been viewed as murders, it would have appeared that a different individual had committed each. Kim was the perfect killing machine.

Kim walked to the basement of the house. Val had the shooting range and training room put in when they lived here together. *When they lived here together;* that was an interesting memory. Closing the soundproof doors behind him, he switched on the lights and prepared to practice his katas.

He removed the Wakizashi from its place on the wall, performing several katas with the razor sharp blade. Thirty minutes later, he wiped the blade down and returned it to its place.

Next was a quick jog around the property that lasted an hour. Then he showered and went to bed. Unless he was on the road, this routine never varied. When on the road, Kim would make arrangements to get his target practice in early at a local gun range. His kata and sword work were done in the hotel room and his run was at the discretion of the locale.

He was feeling the tension within the universe again; he had felt it for days before Val had been killed. He had felt it before but now he recognized it; he knew something was coming and he knew it would involve killing, therefore, he practiced. The tension never went away, but did change; for the last several days it had been increasing... therefore, he practiced.

*****

In Baton Rouge:

After Kim's call, Reverend Mire realized he had three very serious problems. First, several people were inquiring into the history, operations and management of The Willows Resort. Second, Kim Rhodes had known about it before he had. Third, he did not know who was making the inquiries.

Sitting cloistered in the library of his office he thought, *I don't need this right now, too many things hinged on the next two months of successful operation.* His bank account hinged on it, his status within the community—his world—hinged on it. He took another sip of brandy and made up his mind how he would respond to this situation. Purposefully, he pushed the button on his intercom and told his secretary, "Could you have Holly come back in for a moment; I have something to discuss with her." Then he leaned back and unzipped his fly.

Chapter Eighteen

John called me. "We know more about the Corporation than we did with Val Richards. We have to move, but there's still going to be problems. The first is considering an attack/rescue on The Willows. The location is difficult to get into and out of with just that single road. Large scale maps and the intelligence we've gathered show the area surrounding the resort is swampland, complete with mosquitoes, snakes, gators, sink holes and other wonderful 'beasties' that could only survive in a place like this."

John continued, "Turning off of the main highway and going ten miles, a single crossroad intersects from the west. It's built up about four feet above the level of the swamp and covered in a shell and gravel mixture called calechi. The road is one lane and controlled by a gate at an intersection and the command center with the resort. The gate and command center are connected by both landline and radio communications. The command center monitors all communications, perimeters and close-in security and sensors.

"The resort's command center is patched into the local parish sheriff's office and the three area police departments all located within twenty-five miles. The calechi road continues for four miles before it terminates at the man-made island on which the resort's complex is located. At the juncture between the road and the island is an electrically controlled drawbridge that spans a thirty-foot gap between the road and the island."

"My reports say," I interjected, "the resort is a reclaimed section of the swamp that covered approximately 125 acres. This area, like the road, all had to be elevated."

John nodded, "Yes, now the construction and landscaping present an area that was both attractive and functional with the main house dominating the complex. It is three stories tall, the size of a moderate hotel. In the middle of the top floor sets the command center. It's a glass-enclosed structure that has virtually unlimited view of the surrounding swamp. It has command and control functions, as well as fire control capabilities."

"You're saying the road and island are constantly monitored by remote cameras whose fields of vision interlock?"

"Yes, and in addition to visual inputs, motion sensors and pressure sensors, and auditory listening devices are located along the perimeter fencing as well as in all rooms within the resort," John explained. "This allows for taping of the escapades of clientele if they are capable of offering influence in the legal or political arenas, i.e., the blackmail."

"Any good news?"

"Yes." John smiled. "The designers had only made one small mistake and we found it. The glass is obviously bulletproof and the command center has a panoramic view, which totally eliminates the possibility of ground approach going unnoticed. It simply was impossible to move on the resort and not be seen."

I smiled. "Do I sense a 'but?'"

"Yeah, while the command center has an unobstructed view of the property, the surrounding water and the approaching road, it sits directly under the helicopter landing pad. The 'but' is the command center is blind to what is occurring directly over their heads—a mistake that the TAC Team could exploit…if we can just figure out how," John said.

Chapter Nineteen

John and I met in Lake Charles at noon the next day and checked in to the Holiday Inn with adjoining rooms. We set up the computers, white board and flip charts and began the mission planning. By evening, we were both getting pissed having been at this for several hours and still had no way to attack the resort without being seen.

The road was straight, four miles long and any intrusion would be known before we could move fifty yards up the straightaway. Water assault was also out of the question; the water was not deep enough to allow for submersibles or even SCUBA, but it was just deep enough to prevent wading through.

A team would be spotted and trapped out in the open with no maneuverability, no cover, no concealment; not a good choice.

John got up and stretched. He headed to the map; silent for what seemed like minutes, he slowly turned around and smiled. "One if by land and two if by sea, my ass!" he declared to no one. In an obvious connection to the ride of Paul Revere and the approach of the British, he announced, "No, by God, it will be three if by air."

"What in the hell are you talking about?" I asked, pouring another drink.

"Simple," he said, "we cannot attack from the road—we'll be seen and slaughtered, right? We cannot attack from the water—again, no cover and we're dead, right?"

"Right again," I said, still not sure where he was headed.

"What are the three elements of the ancient Greeks?" he asked, with a smile.

"Earth, wind and fire?" I asked, but knew that was a singing group.

"Close, actually the answer is land, sea and air. We fly in," he said, smugly.

"Okay, genius," I said in frustration. "We can't use the road to land; we would be cut to pieces before we could get out of a plane or chopper. There is no place to land on the water, nor can we land on the helo pad or fast rope out. NO COVER! NO CONCEALMENT! NO SURVIVAL!"

"That is absolutely correct," he said, obviously pleased with himself.

"We can't parachute in; even high altitude low opening is out—we are too close to the restricted air space of the nearby nuclear plant," I pointed out.

"That's right," he said, "HALO won't work." He continued to smile.

"All right, I give up, how do we fly in if not by plane, chopper or parachute?"

"A powered paraglider," he said. "It's like a special parachute; the pilot wears a backpack that is nothing but a motor with a propeller. We can takeoff from this road right here and gain as much altitude as we can. Then when we are close enough, cut engines to avoid detection, sail in and land on the damned helo pad. They are easy to fly; direction is changed by pulling on a toggle on the chute's raisers.

"Pull left, you go left; pull right, you go right. Pull down hard with both hands and you stall the forward motion of the chute and land as easily as stepping out of the bath tub. It is perfect." He was on a roll.

"Let me think about this for a minute," I said, moving to the map and picture board. For several minutes we both walked around the table saying nothing. Then it was as though two voices were being used by one mind. The plan came out in a tumble; I honestly don't remember who had which elements. It all swam together, but it would work.

Five men with powered parasails would takeoff from State Road 71 after being dropped off. Four men would head down the parish road to the approach to the resort and knock out the guard shack. Once there, two would unload a four wheeler and prepare to approach the resort. The other two would remain at the intersection of the parish road and the access drive, acting as a rear guard.

Two more squads of two people each would move into easy reach of the resort in high-speed bass boats; not an uncommon sight on the lake. They would appear to simply be fishermen, but would be prepositioned to respond when the assault was initiated. Rescue and retreat would be a little more complicated.

Chapter Twenty

Sheriff Arvin J. O'Malley, in his sixties and retired from public life for six years, was a throw back. A.J. used technology but didn't trust it; computers and gadgets hadn't come along until almost the end of his military career. In twenty years as an Air Force Security Policeman, he knew every aspect of the career field and was good at all of them. His last years were spent as a Flight Chief, not the ideal position for him.

Some folks thought he spent too much time at the local watering hole.

At that time, he was working for David Blaine and, like many of Blaine's subordinates, A.J. developed a sincere respect and affection for "the Boss." Part of that was because Blaine was responsible for A.J. putting the bottle down. Blaine had summoned O'Malley to his office one morning. A.J. was off that day and arrived fifteen minutes late in civilian clothes.

His clothes were rumpled and the stink of alcohol couldn't be disguised by his after shave. Blaine told him to close the door and for the next hour they talked. At the end of the hour, A.J. had made a solemn vow not to drink again and Blaine gave him a promise that he would be allowed to retire with all honor—if the drinking stopped. One year later, MSgt O'Malley retired from active duty with honor.

Blaine gave him a friend's number in West Texas to contact for a job. A.J. felt that the area seemed like the armpit of the world, but it was the best thing that ever happened to him. He hooked up with the Sheriff's Department and broke several big cases in rapid succession.

He wasn't a high-profile investigator, but he was dogged and determined and he was no longer on the bottle. When the Sheriff retired, A.J. was elected and served until his own retirement.

A few months ago, a rancher named Ben Cochran had come to O'Malley's small ranch; his daughter had disappeared. Cochran asked O'Malley to find his daughter. O'Malley asked, "I don't know why you came to me on this. I'd love to help but you know I'm retired?"

Cochran spoke slowly, "I'm asking because you're the most dogged son of a bitch we ever had as Sheriff. I was with you back in '83 when we were looking for that lost kid. You didn't quit, you kept on. You kept up the search when everyone else had given up, you didn't quit. I need someone who won't quit."

"What do you expect me to do?" O'Malley said. "I'm retired. I have no authority."

"I want you to find my daughter, Terri," Cochran said, and turned before O'Malley could see the tear that was about to fall from his eyes. The rancher took a deep breath, wiped his eyes and turned back. O'Malley was reaching for a cup of coffee and pretended he had not seen the man's weakness.

"I know she's alive. I know some bastard took her and I want her back. I'll go get her but I need you to help me find her." O'Malley agreed to help, but his leads were few and led to nowhere.

Then the following week, A.J. got a phone call. "John, its David Blaine." O'Malley unconsciously shifted to a more upright position and said, "Sir, how are you doing?" It was the first time they had talked in ten years.

"I'm doing great. I see you're still in Texas; how are you?"

O'Malley relaxed a little and said, "Yes sir, same place, just retired now." After catching up on the last ten years, Blaine asked if O'Malley knew a man named Ben Cochran. The hair on the back of O'Malley's neck stood up. "Yes Sir. As a matter of fact, I've taken a private case with him trying to find his daughter. She disappeared or to his way of thinking was kidnapped a while back."

Blaine explained that the girl had been recovered and, without a lot of detail, he brought O'Malley up on the raid into Mexico and the rescue of several people, including Cochran's daughter. She was under medical treatment now and Blaine wanted O'Malley to prepare Cochran before he saw his daughter. He was sending some faxed photos.

O'Malley took down some information and hung up. He walked out on the porch and smoked a cigarette before calling Cochran. He thought about what Blaine had said. He snubbed the butt out on a rail and went back inside and dialed the Cochran ranch. O'Malley asked if they could meet. Mr. Cochran asked, "Have you found my daughter?"

"No, but I know where she is. I can tell you she is safe but is not going to be able to come home right now," O'Malley answered. "I need to talk to you before you say anything to your wife or anyone else."

"Okay, Sheriff. Let's meet at the top of Preacher's Hill? You know where that's at, right?"

"I do," O'Malley said. "But I ain't the Sheriff no more."

"You'll be Sheriff to me till the day I die. I'll see you in an hour and I won't talk to anyone till after we've talked."

There were no roads to Preacher's Hill, so O'Malley saddled a horse. O'Malley had pulled pictures of Cochran's daughter off the fax machine and slid them into the saddle bags he carried. He walked out to the barn where the horse, a big buckskin, was tied to the corral fence. He tied on the saddle bags, adjusted his hat and placing his left foot in the stirrup, swung into the saddle.

It was a good day for a ride; the weather was clear and just cool enough to be comfortable. O'Malley rode to the top of Preacher's Hill and saw Cochran. O'Malley dismounted and tied his horse next to Cochran's, untied his saddle bags and walked over to the man. They shook hands. "Ben," O'Malley said, "I wanted to see you before you talked to your wife. I want to tell you what I know and discuss how you can help your daughter when she comes home."

"When can I see her?" Cochran asked.

"If everything goes well, next week. She is in a hospital recovering from her injuries. Physically she'll be fine but she's been through hell." O'Malley opened the saddle bags, handed the pictures to Cochran and walked to the far side of the hill.

He didn't want to embarrass the man by standing there while he looked at the pictures. O'Malley had seen them and felt fury and tears well up in his own eyes. This was the man's daughter and he deserved a moment of privacy.

Cochran thumbed through the photos and walked over to his horse. He rummaged through his own saddle bags until he came up with a bottle of Black Label Jack Daniels and two cigars. He walked over to O'Malley. "I haven't had a drop in fifteen years," he said to O'Malley, as he took a swig and passed the bottle over. "Promise I made to the girl's mother. I was afraid I'd be needing it and I was right."

He rubbed his coat sleeve across his eyes and coughed to hide the anguish in his voice. "What som' bitch did this to my little girl?" He puffed on the cigar but the smoke couldn't hide the pure cold fury of the rancher's eyes.

O'Malley lit a cigar and acted like he had taken a small swig of whiskey before passing it back to Cochran. O'Malley knew better than to swallow the whiskey, he'd fought too hard and too long to get that monkey off his back but he also knew Cochran wouldn't notice.

"One thoroughly dead som' bitch," O'Malley said. "I can't tell you very much, but I can promise that you never have to worry about the bastard coming back."

"For sure?"

"For absolutely sure. Som' bitch lost his head, literally."

Cochran nodded, "Who got 'em?"

O'Malley shook his head. "Can't tell you and you can't ask no more questions. This is a dead subject. I am way over the line telling you this much. I need your word that your questions stop here with me today; it'll mean trouble for me if they don't."

Cochran nodded and took another drink. "Sheriff, I'd never cause you no trouble. You found my girl and I am forever in your debt." He looked out across the prairie for a long time then turned to O'Malley and said, "It's a dead issue. My girl's coming home; the bastard that did this to her is dead and gone. She has a life to live and by God she'll have a good one."

"You okay?"

Cochran screwed the top on the whiskey and stowed it back in his saddle bag. He mounted his horse and spun the horse to face O'Malley. "Sheriff," he said, "my baby was taken, but I knew she was alive somewhere. Today, a good man told me she is okay and coming home. I've got a lot to make up with that kid and now I've got the time to do it. We'll be okay, but remember, I owe you and I take that seriously."

Cochran spun his horse and rode off before O'Malley could speak. A.J. watched the man ride off, turned to his horse and mounted. He rode up next to the single tree on the hill and used it to stub out the cigar. Then he rode back to his ranch the way he had come, but on this leg of the trip, he whistled.

Chapter Twenty-One

Evening traffic in Houston means any trip takes longer than normal. By the time Pam came home, I had showered and was nearly dressed for our evening out. Two hours later, we took our seats at the small formal dinner party held by one of her business associates on his boat in Galveston Harbor.

The insurance broker raised his glass of Scotch and I saluted with my Jack and Seven. After dinner, Pam and I excused ourselves for a moonlit walk around the deck; it was the last relaxation I would have for a long time.

The next morning I called John. "Hey Boy, what is going on in Baton Rouge?"

"Everything is going pretty well," John said. "What's up with you?"

"I talked to David Blaine this morning. We need to talk. What are you doing this weekend?"

"Sounds like I'm coming to see you," he said.

Once we had that set up, I realized it was time to pick another mission planner since Hank Devlin had dropped out. It needed to be someone with a military or high-level, police intelligence background; the ideal candidate would have both.

David Blaine had offered us a type of governmental sanction; that meant covert support by elements of the Federal Government was now at my disposal. I had discussed the situation with Blaine when I was in Palm Springs last month.

He had said, "Doc, I don't see this as a major obstacle. You will have all of the intelligence support you need for planning this mission." I told him that was great, but I need a pair of boots on the ground for operational interpretation of the Intel.

He told me, "I see this mainly a problem for working with someone new, but I don't see that it will hurt the mission."

I agreed and asked, "Any ideas as to who?"

Blaine thought for a moment and then said, "Maybe... A guy named Jed Kovak, former Marine pilot, DEA and he's tough, smart and un-compromising."

"Sounds like an asshole." I smirked.

"Yeah, he is. You two ought to get along great and he's down in your neck of the woods. I'll have him contact you directly and you two can start trying to see who can piss higher up the tree. Once you have your relationship defined, you'll find he's damn good at what he does."

I had smiled and said, "Boss, sounds like you're saying, 'He's a nice person once you get to know him,' when what you mean is, 'He's a dickhead but you'll get used to it.'"

"Yep!"

"Sounds like you know him pretty well."

"I do and I like him," Blaine admitted. "You need to visit with him yourself though if you're going to have faith in what he gives you. I'll have him call you."

*****

Later, I received a fax from Blaine. It was a condensed dossier on Ko-vak. He said Kovak would provide me with a full dossier.

Jed Kovak, Call Sign:
Age: 34
Current location: Houston, TX
Physicals: White, Male, 6' 1", Brown/green

Military: Class of 76 USMC Charlie Company 4th Platoon 102nd OCC TBS class 5-77 Quantico USMC firearms instructor 1979 (VMFAT-101-Yuma AZ) VMFA-314, VMFA-531, favorite task, flying intercepts inverted (F-4N, F-4J). FAC, NGF spotter, Artillery FO, Squadron training officer, NBC officer, assistant base Ops Officer attended College Dart, Tyndall AFB FL 1980, attended Red Flag 81-1 and 81-2 at Nellis AFB, separated December 1981 March 1982, went to work at Buddy Line Divers, Mt. Pleasant, S.C. (owner was a sheep dipped SF MSGT).

All ratings up to master diver trainer, taught diving students at the citadel. 22-ish diver specialty ratings trained Charleston SC police dive and rescue team 1982/83 Commercial diver, factory trained scuba gear repair guy, safety diver for movies "Rear View Mirror" and "North and South". Dive store was front for supplying Hondurans with dive gear and training during Nicaraguan incursion 82/83.

Background: Extensive training in weapons, explosives, attended jungle warfare school at Ft. Sherman Panama. 1988 built up DEA San Diego Clan Lab Enforcement Team #1.

Weapons: Extensive

Chapter Twenty-Two

The modest wood frame house sat on an equally modest street. Like the other homes, it was singularly unimposing, serviceable, but plain. It conformed, it was normal. The house, the street and the town had all been picked for that quality—normalcy. In the last census, the population had topped 30,000 for the first time. Nothing stood out; it was perfectly suited to its owner. The neighbors knew only that he traveled a lot in his computer business.

In his mid to late forties and of average height and weight, like the house, the street, and the town, nothing about him stood out. Blaming his lack of socializing on his business travels, he did not participate in the civic clubs that made up the majority of social events within the town.

He attended a Mosque in a neighboring town and, as far as anyone could tell, he never had visitors. He was a solitary individual who kept to himself and bothered no one.

He was polite and spoke to his neighbors if they were outside, but he did not visit them and they did not visit him. The first floor of 635 Kelly Street was much like its owner—modest and assuming. There was a living room with a couch and old-style entertainment center, a bathroom and a study.

The second floor was a different story all together. Several walls had been taken out to create a loft effect. Contrary to the rest of the house, it was expensive and elegant in the extreme. That floor contained more computer power than the entire city possessed. This was necessary to his work... and his hobby. Without the computer, his career would not have been possible.

He'd built the computer himself and constructed it to function as the master communication system equivalent to any Fortune 500 Information Management System. He could make contact anywhere around the world; he had one-way video hook ups. He could see his clients and his victims but no one ever saw him; he had access to their computer systems. His little discovery almost thirty years ago was the secret to his success.

The ability to access a computer without the operator being aware of it had not even been conceived by the great minds of the computer industry of the time.

Thirty years ago, he was a young student named Earl Levant, one of those shy kids who had no direction until he ended up in the high school computer lab. All that changed the day a computer mistake had sent him to that class. Back then, computers were large and slow.

Earl walked in to Mr. Robinette's class that first day and something "clicked" in the universe. Earl had found his place. Earl understood computers; he thought in the same terms that they operated. In four weeks, he had surpassed the teacher's limited knowledge and began spending every evening in the library.

It was 1969 and the personal computer rage was still years away but several libraries in town, and the local university, had computers that the public and students could use for a small fee. Within a year, Earl was writing his own computer programs; initially simple programs, but as he gained in understanding, the programs became more and more complex.

Upon graduation, Earl went to work in the rapidly developing computer industry. Few of his co-workers had his experience with computers or his ability. He'd work with a particular company or group until he'd learned everything they could teach him then he'd move on.

Chapter Twenty-Three

Earl took equipment from every company he worked for; nothing big, just enough that he could work at home on some of his projects. It started innocently enough. He once asked his supervisor if he could have some of the equipment that had been junked out and was headed for the trash bin.

The supervisor had said, "Sure, the stuff is junk to me." Earl took the equipment apart, found the problem and reassembled it. When he turned it on, it worked. He converted one entire wall of his family garage to his own computer lab, spending hours there. Each job he had ended up contributing not only experience but hardware for his lab.

During this period, Earl became intrigued with the Muslim faith. It appealed to many of the lost, the disenfranchised and to those who had been dominated by others their whole life. He studied the Koran and began attending Mosque. Hiding his true identity, he took the Muslim name, Abbu Nemiah, known only to his Muslim friends and he kept the two aspects of his developing life separate. He kept building his own computer and over the next ten years was able to upgrade it to the point that in 1979, he was ready.

1979 was the year that Earl Levant died. At twenty-seven, he still looked much the same as he had in high school. While still slight of build, his confidence level had changed; with computers he had found his own place. He had met the right people as the computer industry evolved... he had just made the greatest discovery of his life while working on a particularly troublesome program.

Earl realized that he was able to gain access to the workings of the computer without the computer being aware of his presence. He had created the first of what later "hackers" would call a worm.

Shortly after discovering his "secret," his supervisor brought him in for a review. Edward Donnelly was an arrogant, self-centered little bastard who no one liked. In his normal condescending manner, this supervisor advised Earl that company bonuses this year were restricted to "those singular individuals with a high sense of dedication to the company and above average productivity. And that does not include you."

Donnelly thanked him for his time and ensured Earl that if he would spend his time more productively, next year's review would certainly be better. Earl knew how bonuses worked; senior management decided on a dollar figure they could afford to be given out. Mid-level managers were tasked with distributing that amount amongst the workforce.

The fewer number of individuals selected for the bonus, the greater the bonus for those individuals. Donnelly, unaffectionally known as "Fat Eddie" by his workers, simply reduced the number of individuals selected, gave them a predetermined percent of increase and pocketed the rest.

Fat Eddie was a bully. He intimidated rather than managed and he instilled fear rather than inspiring loyalty. After his review, Earl continued to sit in front of Fat Eddie's desk. "Is there anything else?" Donnelly finally asked.

"I'm just trying to figure out why I'm not getting a bonus," Earl said, quietly.

After a moment Donnelly said, "Am I going to have a problem with you young man?"

Earl said, quietly, "No sir, but I was counting on that money to help me buy some new equipment. I don't think this is fair."

Donnelly stood up and leaned on the desk with both hands and said, "Son, the world is not fair. Our internal surveillance of your terminal shows an inordinate amount of time doing private research. Research done on company time for private interests is against policy and could result in your termination. Do I make myself clear?"

"Perfectly," Earl said, and left the office. He went to his computer typed in some commands which brought up a special screen. He printed the screen and sat there pondering what to do with the information; a record of every porn site that Fat Eddy had visited in the past three months. It was extensive and showed visits lasting from a few seconds to as much as thirty minutes.

Earl knew he could send it up channel to higher management, but that would mean an investigation. It was possible someone would discover who had tracked the information and that the tracking was just as illegal as what Fat Eddy had done and would result in both of them being terminated.

Earl went back to Fat Eddy's office and knocked on the door. Quietly, Earl said, "Sir, may I speak freely?"

Fat Eddy thought, *Okay, here comes the whining for the raise,* but he said, "Earl, I've given you my decision and it is final."

Again, Earl said, "Sir, may I speak freely?"

Exasperated, Fat Eddy leaned back in his chair and put both hands on the back of his neck before saying, "Go away Mister, I'm a busy man." Then he smiled. "I'll give you two minutes."

Earl said, quietly, "Thank you." Without a further word, he slid the printout across Fat Eddy's desk. Donnelly leaned forward and picked up the printout. His face went from normal to red then to a ghostly paleness. Donnelly stood up and walked to the door and closed it.

"Where did you get this?" he asked.

Earl sensed the shift in power and said, "That is not important Mr. Donnelly. What is important is that you have the only copy, for right now. As far as I am concerned, you have the only copy that will ever be printed."

Donnelly was sweating. "That's good Earl," he said. "I appreciate that, this information could be interpreted incorrectly and create a terrible misunderstanding. I appreciate you bringing this to me. You haven't shared this with anyone, have you?"

Earl smiled and said, "Certainly not, Sir, at least not yet."

Donnelly nodded his understanding and said, "I see Earl. I understand."

Earl had never seen Fat Eddy so submissive and decided to push the point. "No Sir, I don't think you do. I need your assurances on a couple of matters before I leave. Number one, about the bonus we discussed a moment ago, I believe that an amount twice what I expected when I came in is appropriate. Second, I agree to leave this company twelve months from today. I will give you a signed, undated letter of resignation.

"During that period of time, I will be assigned to a special project under your direct supervision. My position will be upgraded and I will receive a raise on top of the bonus I just received. While on that special project, I will work on nothing for this company.

"You will reassign all of my current duties to other programmers and I will have unlimited computer access and support. At the end of that year, I will leave and you simply report the project was fruitless. Oh and by the way when I leave, I will expect a glowing letter of recommendation."

Donnelly swelled and his face turned red under his short, cropped, flattop haircut. The stubble on his jawline seemed to glow; he was not used to being out maneuvered. "Further," Earl said, "you and I don't ever need to speak of this again. In fact, we don't need to speak at all. If my demands are not met to the letter, if I have any issues or problems from you in the next twelve months, if there is anything negative in my personnel records or if any unexpected layoffs occur that affect me—I will ensure a copy of this and 'other' information arrives on the company President's desk the next day."

Earl stood. Donnelly nodded his understanding, heavy drops of sweat falling to the desk top. Earl turned and walked out. Earl was sweating also, but it was from excitement. He enjoyed power, it was exhilarating. He enjoyed watching Donnelly squirm, and was particularly proud of the comment about "other information."

That had been a spontaneous bolt of brilliance. He saw that Donnelly was trapped and he had closed in for the kill. Donnelly had no idea what the "other information" might be, but obviously he could not take any chances. Earl realized there was far more to this man than he had thought of, more skeletons at least.

At the end of the day, Earl went home and turned on the computer. He had planted his cookie on Donnelly's home PC weeks ago, but for whatever reason, never accessed it. Tonight he did and found why Donnelly was so pliable. Edward Donnelly was obsessed with pornography about little boys; Fat Eddy was a pedophile. Earl smiled.

The next day Earl's cubicle was moved to a private office and Donnelly made an announcement about the fine work Earl had been doing and that he was now assigned to a special project. Earl's first attempt at blackmail had worked and worked well.

Over the months and years to come, he would refine his technique; but for now, the bonus and the raise along with his special project was exactly what he had wanted.

It offered him the chance to upgrade his home system and continue to refine his cookie. His company was one of the first to start experimentation with home computer cameras and teleconferencing. Earl realized that his cookie worked on those programs as well. From the time he left Fat Eddy's office that day, until October 8, Earl had refined his plan. He'd already come up with the Abbu Nemiah identity. With Fat

Eddy's acquiescence and protection, development of the plan and the improvements on the cookie were progressing at an almost exponential rate.

Earl's research showed him something else; America was inhabited by a society of perverts. His cookie allowed him access to every key stroke written and every site visited for every computer that was now infected with his cookie. Each day the list grew, and each week his analysis showed beneath the veneer of civilization, there were a bunch of sick bastards with fantasies that could have only generated from nightmares.

Earl had led a sheltered life; he'd never seen a girly magazine or a blue movie. Past puberty, he'd never had a sexual experience or a girl-friend and never really had a desire for either. It just seemed like too much work for too little reward.

After he joined the workforce, he listened while co-workers bitched and complained about their wives and husbands. Earl did not under-stand why anyone would live with someone they didn't like. He'd de-cided long ago that "love was bull shit." Since he had never had love, he didn't miss it. Since he had never had sex, he didn't crave it.

Chapter Twenty-Four

On October 8, 1984, Paul Levant, Earl's father, left the local bar late and drunk as usual. Paul was a big man; six foot, two inches and about 235 pounds, and had worked hard all of his life. He had buried Earl's mother when Earl was in high school. "Useless bitch," he slurred out loud as he walked the six blocks from the bar to the house. "She never cared about me," Paul mumbled as he moved uneasily down the street. "She never loved me, just that whelp of hers."

Paul Levant was not Earl's real father. He had met Helen, and fallen instantly in love. When Helen confided that she was pregnant, and the father would not marry her, Paul had thought, "This is my lucky day." He married Helen, a woman who normally would not have looked twice at the blue-collar Paul Levant. She was his treasure and he considered himself to be the luckiest man in the world.

He worshipped her and they seemed well suited. Seven months later she gave birth to Earl. Paul had wanted to name the boy Paul, but she insisted on Earl. Tonight, Paul's anger was increasing with each step and each memory. "Earl," he murmured. "What a name. I know she named him after the bastard who made him." From the moment the baby was born, things began to change. It did not take long for Paul to realize he had been used.

Helen poured all of her love into the boy. Although Paul tried to be a real father to the boy, it had never worked. Helen always intervened between Paul and Earl. The kid didn't like sports or working on cars. He didn't like anything that Paul knew how to do. They grew further and further apart.

Gradually, Helen, a once beautiful woman, turned into a frump. Her fine figure disappeared under pounds of flab. Once meticulous about her appearance, she seldom even put on makeup in those later years. She complained all of the time about everything and most particularly how life had cheated her of her own life. She watched soap operas and lived out her fantasies on the small screen; finally, she just died.

Paul had stumbled home one night from the bar and found her on the floor in the living room with the Earl sitting there holding her hand. He stood for a moment trying to figure out why the stupid cow was on the floor. He saw the boy crying and realized what had happened and laughed as he bent over her big bloated body.

He felt relief, the constant bitching was over. Now, maybe he could begin to have a real life. For a moment he looked at her body and thought of how beautiful she had been and how lucky he had thought himself to have her. Then his drunken stupor returned and he spit on her and walked out of the room to call the coroner.

Earl watched the man he called father spit on his dead mother and vowed one day to kill him. It would take ten years to fulfill that vow. At 10:38 P.M., October 8, 1984, Paul Levant stumbled up his driveway and headed to the garage. He hadn't planned it, things just sort of happened.

One minute he was standing in the doorway looking at all of this computer crap and the next minute, he picked up a long pipe and began smashing everything that Earl had built. On his third swing, he smashed through the protective covering on one piece of equipment and buried the pipe in the guts of the machine.

The machine fought back and sent an electrical charge up the metal pipe and into Paul Levant's body. His body froze, his muscles contracted. Instead of dropping the pipe, the electricity made his hands grip the pipe even harder. His face contracted and struggled to get out of the current, but he couldn't move. He couldn't call out or even scream.

His mind continued to function throughout all of it. He could feel the current cooking him from the inside out. He could smell his burning flesh. He knew it all until finally death granted him peace.

What Paul had not known was that Earl had heard the turmoil and was watching. Paul didn't know Earl was standing just five feet away in the doorway watching him die. After a long time, Paul's body fell over and the connection was broken.

Earl walked over and pulled a cigarette pack from Paul's pocket; it had a pack of matches in the cellophane wrapper. He tipped a plastic gas can over; five gallons of gas poured out across the floor and ran under Paul's body.

Earl walked to the door of the garage and looked out. No one was watching or had heard anything. He turned and walked back to Paul's body; he stood there for a long moment before spitting on his father's corpse. Earl lit the cigarette and walked back toward the house.

From just beyond the door of the garage, he flipped the lighted cigarette into the garage. He stepped inside the house just as the explosion tore the night.

Fire investigators later ruled it an accidental death due to a combination of alcohol, stupidity and the accidental spilling of gasoline. Obviously, Paul Levant had returned home drunk, knocked over the gas can and wrecked the computer equipment belonging to his son. Sometime during or after the electrocution, a spark must have ignited the gasoline.

When the insurance paid out and Paul's estate had been settled, Earl had just under $250,000. He sold the house which gave him another $35,000. Earl took two suitcases: one with his clothes and the other with his computer working tools and some notes.

He bought a one way bus ticket to Oklahoma City and spent two weeks there making plans. He visited the library and had cheap access to a computer. With the aid of that computer, he formulated an audacious plan. He carefully selected the most innocuous location he could find to live in and work out of.

His alter identity of Abbu Nemiah, now had computer generated papers which validated that identify; Earl now seized to exist. Finding the perfect street in the perfect town, Abbu Nemiah began setting up his consulting business and his master plan. He purchased several hard drives and within two weeks, he had everything functioning just the way he wanted it.

Within two months, he had reactivated the cookies he had already planted and began amassing a sizeable fortune. Six months later, he figured out how to implant the command cookie on websites so that each time the website was accessed by a PC, the cookie would install itself through the connection.

Within a few years, the world of the computer expanded significantly and the internet was linked to virtually all homes in the U.S. That's when the money really started coming in and an idea was born.

Chapter Twenty-Five

When the TAC Team was first formed, there had been a specific mission and a clear objective. We invaded Mexico, covertly rescued innocent victims, and returned to the U.S. alive. During that operation, we identified bank accounts owned by people tied to the Corporation and drained them. That "creative financing" funded the first "activation" of the TAC Team and set up the Blue Feather Foundation to care for some of those victims.

Now, with the infusion of funds from certain "unidentified governmental" agencies, the TAC Team was solvent. We were an "unofficial and anonymous" team that handled what could not, or would not, be handled by conventional authorities. We fixed "the unfixable, repaired the unrepairable, and did what no one else could or would do."

The phone rang; it was Jed Kovak. We talked for an hour. Pam entered the room. "Honey," I said, "Jed Kovak just called back, he's coming over this evening."

"Okay. What do you need from me?" she asked.

"Nothing special, we'll order out tonight," I said, then went out to straighten up the War Room.

Kovak's car pulled in the drive a little before 5:00 P.M.; I walked out to meet him. He was a big man, over six feet tall and well over 200 pounds. His light brown hair was cut close and he looked like a cop or a military man. His handshake was firm and he had that quick, but deadly, sense of humor often associated with cops and the military... and yes, Kovak was just a little cocky.

"Colonel Blaine said you were a bit of an asshole," Kovak began. "That true?"

"Yep," I answered with a straight face. "He said you could be one also; that true?"

Kovak stopped in his tracks for a moment, apparently thinking. "Yeah, come to think of it, I guess I can be."

I smiled. "Good, we'll get along just fine then."

I introduced Kovak to Pam then we headed to the War Room. He opened his briefcase and began spreading the contents on the desk. "First of all, we have a major problem," Kovak said. "As I understand this operation, it actually started in Louisiana several weeks ago. A new player, the Reverend Henry Mire, was the target."

"Our initial look at him was focused on this, The Willows Resort," I said, pointing to the location on the map. "We are planning an operation there."

Kovak shook his head. "No you're not; the latest Intel report just came in. Problem number one, The Willows Resort is no longer. I got a call from Blaine while I was driving over. It appears that when you started sniffing around, someone got spooked and everything changed, and I mean it changed on a dime."

"What? What the hell are you talking about?" I said, leaning forward in my chair.

"Don't have all of the details but according Blaine, the resort was abandoned two days ago. Apparently you guys didn't have a full appreciation of Mire's network. As soon as you began making inquiries, the bad guys found out about it and shifted to the west coast. It seems that The Willows was going to be quite an operation, but those plans were dropped like a hot potato. This understandably pissed off several of the local politicians, not to mention it cost them several millions in already expended funds and decimated their anticipated returns on investments."

"But... but..." I didn't even know what to say.

"No buts about it," Kovak said. "The Willows Resort is standing empty and everything, and I mean everything, in it has been removed. Apparently, someone in that operation had met the 'good ol' boys' from Louisiana and arranged financing for The Willows Resort."

"Wow," I said, and stood up. "We must have really shaken someone's comfort zone."

Kovak agreed. "We're not sure what their plan is at this point but we're interested because several of the main players have shown up on our scopes before. Colonel Blaine and his advisors have determined that the super structure of what you and your team ran into last time is, in fact, a front for a clandestine operation with ties to the Middle East. You were correct, at least in part of your theory. I believe that it's nothing more than a criminal operation with ties to international terrorist organizations."

I said, "So if it swims with ducks…"

Kovak smiled and said, "Damn thing's probably a duck. Anyway, that is the general thinking. I want to see how many parts of this operation we can link together before we make any moves."

I thought for a moment. "Let me play this out in my head for a minute."

"Think I'll go hit the can while you do that." When he returned, Kovak saw a look of consternation on my face. "What?" he asked.

"I'm trying to figure it out."

"Figure out what?"

"What your call sign should be," Doc said, with a smile.

"Jed, the Fed," Kovak said. "I got stuck with that when I was in DEA Intel."

"Jed, the Fed, it is," I said. "I called Blaine while you were in the can. Looks like you and I have a trip planned to California."

"Okay, what else?" Kovak asked.

"That's it for right now," I said. "Let me layout the plan we had, it is possible some of it could still be viable." We worked well into the night. When Jed left, I could tell he was excited to be back in the mix of things. The more obscure the process, the better he seemed to like it.

Late the next evening the phone rang and I answered, "Hello."

"Sign on to your email and prepare to download some files," Jed said. "I think I found the info you were looking for. Call me back on the cell after you've had the chance to read it."

"Roger that," I said, and went to the computer and soon had hard copies in hand. An hour later, I sat back, shook my head and dialed Jed's phone number. He answered on the first ring. "Well?" he asked.

"Yeah, listen you did a good job. What's the next step?"

"Don't understand the question," Kovak said. "You know what needs to be done; what the hell are we waiting for?"

Chapter Twenty-Six

Earl Levant had stumbled onto his greatest discovery while trying to come up with a way for computers to debug their own programs. He figured if he could implant a program within the computer that would operate independently of the computer, it could act like a system mechanic and keep the system performing correctly.

Computers are actually very simple machines; everything operationally in them is based on only two digits: a zero or a one. Programs effectively arrange the zeros and ones in sequences that become amazing complex processes, but it remains a simple collection of zeros and ones.

Earl had tapped into the command structure and told the computer how to do what he wanted done. It worked but there was added benefits that Earl had never counted on. His program worked like a cookie, but the computer had no record this cookie ever existed; and this cookie gave a remote operator, such as Earl, unlimited access to the computer with complete recall of all its actions.

Unlike a virus or worm, this cookie waited for instructions from its creator. In the early days, the cookie was primitive and unstable. However, after three years, Earl had refined the cookie to the point of stable sophistication. He named his creation the Cookie Monster.

Now as Abbu Nemiah, he had put the cookie into all computers that he had access to over the years. This included every company he worked for as well as computers he worked on for clients. Since 1984, he had managed to work for each of the biggest producers of computer programs and buried the cookie in their software. He even designed a way to have the cookie implanted in future programs and updates would take place after he left that company.

Earl had never been particularly interested in pornography; for Abbu, however, that was a different story. Pornography had become the foundation of Abbu's fortune and the platform for his first operation, his first step into the holy war called Jihad.

Prior to the advent of the internet, pornography was a hidden activity. Young men had to know which newsstand carried the serious stuff. Otherwise, they would be limited to girly magazines. When the internet came about, the porno masters saw a way to make a killing and so did Abbu.

Abbu's computer software company was now worth millions, housed in an office building in New York City and traded on the stock exchange. Virtually all of the porno sites in the early days of the internet had used Abbu's software to set up. His software enabled them to virtually eliminate the middle man and could control, update and correct their sites as they wished.

No one knew that imbedded in the software was Abbu's cookie. No one knew that the profits from this company were being used to help finance an invasion across the borders of America and its eventual death as a country.

By 1992, the internet had become a reality; almost every home had at least one computer and nearly every office in the country was linked. Abbu's cookie tracked every fantasy and perversion of his unseen audiences.

Abbu was clinical in his observations of the predilections of other human beings; analytical in realizing that this silly obsession shared by so many could be used to get him the money he so desperately needed. Their cravings proved to his benefit; Abbu learned people were obsessed with it.

Each day the number of hits to porno sites he monitored increased. Each day, the number of computers infected with Earl's cookie increased; then came the computer cams.

Within just three years of what was thought futuristic, the video phones of the science fiction of his youth had become reality. For hours, Abbu surveyed his collection of "data ports" as he called them, his computer sorting information based on certain demographics. His goal was money and he had learned the best way to get money was to have people give it to him.

His computer business was growing and highly successful, but it would never give Abbu the independence and the power he was now craving; blackmail, however, would. Abbu wanted to know about that person and what resources he or she might have.

For example, a church youth minister viewing kiddy porn became an excellent source of regular income. A politician doing the same thing became a source of power that Abbu could tap into when needed. A public figure with secret fantasies would become a client, if Abbu found a way to cater to those fascinations.

He set out to create exactly that place; an exclusive private club. His first attempt was in Indonesia; a predominately Muslim country where "good Arabs" could go to exercise their fantasies. He wanted to make all of his mistakes outside of America and in jurisdictions that could be bought off if necessary. It worked and worked well. Making contact through intermediaries, Abbu established a network of operatives that bought property, constructed other clubs and ran the operation.

Abbu made it lucrative for his managers; operational costs came off the top and then profits were split on a fifty-fifty basis.

Japanese business men, who were notoriously chauvinistic, were thrilled to have blond Caucasians become their love slaves. While many

Orientals and representatives of other non-white cultures wanted desperately to possess Caucasians, that possession had never before occurred in a way which offered both ultimate pleasure and ultimate protection.

Abbu's clubs offered both. Drugs, sex and perversions of any taste were presented, not in back rooms, shadowy alleys or fumbling couplings in the dark. Now, they were promoted, exploited and presented as they had never been before; it was addictive.

Likewise, when supposedly devout Arabic businessmen and politicians from places such as the United Arab Emirates, Saudi Arabia and Uzbekistan, just to name a few, traveled to America, they found an opportunity to work on the dark side of sexual liaisons.

Of particular interests was the "purchasing" of the virginity of teens and women for a price, as well as the darker sides of rape and bondage. Often, after a session or two of aberrant sexual exploitation, they would return home as pious as when they left. After all, what happens overseas stays overseas.

Abbu provided a way to explore any fantasy that could be imagined. Since he was not interested in the fantasy aspects of sexual contact, since he did not crave the stimulation, he had the objectivity a psychologist has when examining a patient; he realized that fantasy realization brought a degree of desensitizing.

The same "rush" would never again be experienced as it was the first time that fantasy was realized. Like drugs, the stimulant effect was optimum only in the beginning. Gradually, what had been fantasy became reality. Reality was never as totally consuming as the fantasy and the stimulation had to be increased. In other words, like illegal drugs, the "dose" had to be repeated.

Also, these doses quickly began coming in closer proximity to each other; doses had to be increased to have similar impact. Like illegal drugs, the drug of choice eventually would have to be changed to get the same effect. Through it all, the addict paid for the fantasy; and for the addiction.

Then he had been contacted by Val Richards who had a growing network of resorts that could provide an even greater playground. Combining the necessary elements of a Roman orgy, a rock conference, a high school seduction, an incestuous relationship, a fumbling first attempt or a murderous rage all in one, Val's resorts provided it all.

During their first year of operation, a new opportunity presented itself in the form of Hiram Jenkins; a school teacher from central Kansas. He was tall and cadaver slender with mousey blond hair, grown long on the sides and not at all on the top of his pale, bald pate. Hiram taught third grade in a small town and frequently took trips all over the country and brought back wonderful slide shows that he shared with the students.

Hiram, a popular teacher and deacon in the local church, was also a serial killer.

Chapter Twenty-Seven

Hiram began killing when he was a child. For years, neighborhood pets would disappear from time to time. The first few were found, some dissected and two cats had been set on fire. It caused such a stink that young Hiram realized he must hide the bodies of his victims.

Luckily, there was a wooded area next to a drainage ditch behind his house. That became his cemetery. For years, Hiram would stalk a pet, figure out how to make the snatch and then steal the animal.

He had to wait until his mother was gone on a weekend trip with one of her many male friends. Hiram's father had left years before. In those early years, he thought his mother's many male friends were auditioning for a permanent position then realized they were simply using his mother.

During this period of his life, Hiram was able to fulfill his sick fantasies on cats and dogs. Eventually, he realized he was not getting the same "kick" that he used to get during his stalks, captures and killings. That changed on his fifteenth birthday; Hiram left the house and walked along the drainage ditch.

Again, his mother failed to remember or even acknowledge his birthday. Hiram walked to the corner store and bought himself a cupcake then went to the ditch to watch the stagnant water and the birds that hunted for minnows in its nasty depths. He had been feeling the "tension" for several days now.

This tension always preceded one of his animal killings. It had built, and he knew it was time to begin stalking. As it got stronger, Hiram worked out the details of the capture. When it reached its dénouement, he would snatch an animal and subject it to all of the horrors that inhabited Hiram's dark soul.

This time, however, there was no animal that captured his attention; this time he decided would be different. Sitting there looking at the stagnant ditch munching his birthday cupcake, he decided to hunt a human. He finished the cupcake and walked the length of the ditch. He had gone about a mile when he saw his target; a bum, a hobo.

The bum had made camp near the ditch on a piece of wooded land about an acre in size. It was surrounded by a small industrial park that was closed because it was a Sunday. Hiram walked up to the bum and spoke, "Hey sir, how are you doing?"

The bum looked up from his cooking pot with a blurry, alcohol stare. He looked back down at the pot and said, "Can't have none, don't have enough."

Hiram laughed. "Oh, I don't want any of that. I wanted to know if you wanted to come home with me and have Sunday dinner."

The bum stared at the boy and said, "For real?"

"Sure, I live just over there," Hiram said, as he pointed. When the bum turned to look in that direction, Hiram stabbed him in the neck with the Phillips screw driver he'd carried in his back pocket for three days. He stabbed the man again and again in the chest and stomach. When the old bum finally fell to the ground, whimpering, Hiram stabbed him until he was dead.

Hiram looked around, as soon as the red haze that colored his vision had passed. No one was around, no one had seen him; he had killed a human. Hiram saw that his clothes were covered in blood, the bum's blood, his privates were wet. A stain was seeping through his jeans. He thought he had peed on himself, but it didn't smell like urine. He then realized he had experienced his first orgasm.

He smiled to himself and said to the bum, "I came when you went." Hiram put rocks in the dead man's pockets and rolled him into the waters of the drainage ditch. Then he calmly walked back along the ditch and to his house. He cleaned the screwdriver off and put it on a shelf high in his closet. He took his clothes off, ran them through the washing machine cycle twice and with a dose of bleach. Then he showered. Hiram felt wonderful, powerful.

When Hiram eventually went to one of the resorts, he enjoyed the more violent forms of pornographic images and sex. It had not taken long for Abbu to realize there was a way to take advantage of Hiram's predilection. He also realized there was an untapped and growing harvest of potential victims for people like Hiram.

Pedophiles, for the past several years, had been using the World Wide Web to "troll" for young victims. Abbu knew the same web could be used somewhat differently.

To Abbu, this was simply business; he understood computers and how to make money. He understood power and how to use it. Abbu did not understand human feelings like guilt or remorse. Abbu took a tremendous chance; he made personal contact with Hiram. The purpose of that contact?

Abbu had come to realize that eventually all things change; he wanted an "ace in the hole." Kim Rhodes was a killer; Val Richards was also a killer. Abbu was not; the next best thing was for him to enlist a killer for himself; Hiram became that killer.

Chapter Twenty-Eight

Kovak had started by sending a torrent of information, which I tried to collect and assess the significance, but frankly I was getting somewhat overwhelmed with the sheer volume of information. I called Jed and said, "Before we head to California, let me ask you something. I work a lot better with a face-to-face construct. How about bringing over all of your info and help me figure out what we need to do with all of this crap?"

"No problem, Doc, I was going to suggest the same thing. I'll see you in two hours."

"Great, I appreciate it."

*****

Now in Palm Springs, Jed said to Blaine, "Our intelligence says there's a newly established compound facility in California that appears to be functioning as a port of call. A yacht launches from the marina behind it and makes trips to undisclosed rally points several miles past the boundary of the U.S. territorial waters. These rendezvous are with a small freighter that has been bought and refurbished on the inside into a pleasure palace, reminiscent of the reign of the Roman Emperor Caligula.

"The ship was purchased from China by a small shipping company out of Mindanao in the southern Philippines. This shipping company is actually a holding company, which is owned by the multibillionaire son of a member of the Saudi Arabian aristocracy. The guy's name is Osama Bin Laden."

Blaine interjected, "I know of him, he's the seventeenth son of a Saudi construction mogul, Bin Laden, who went to Afghanistan to help fight against the Russian invasion. He formed a cell of freedom fighters called al-Qaeda, which means The Rock, and did significant damage to the Russian forces. Bin Laden is described as a radical, fundamentalist Muslim. After Afghanistan, his name continued to surface in links to terrorist attacks throughout the Middle East, including some on Americans."

I interrupted, "David, wait a minute. Let me understand this. You're saying that this operation is for sure somehow linked to illegal immigration, pornography and international terrorism?"

Blaine nodded. "This is exactly what I'm saying. We're not sure how but there is a connection. This ship was gutted and completely restored. On the outside, she looks like a small freighter flying the Panamanian flag. On the inside, it looks like a five-star hotel.

"There are papers transferring ownership from the shipping company in Mindanao, through what we assume are three dummy companies, ending up with a purchase by a representative of the compound; sounds excessive, but on the surface it's not illegal. Here is where it becomes a little more of a rub; the ship never docks."

"What do you mean it never docks?" Warlord asked.

Blaine said, "Let me be more accurate; it never docks in this country. The small freighter, now called the Canary, moves back and forth from Mindanao to China to Indonesia and then just off the coast of southern California. It never enters U.S. territorial waters; therefore, we cannot legally examine or board the Canary. Let me give you the rest of the briefing then I'll come back to the Canary in a minute and tie all of this up.

"The Canary routinely has visitors who are transported from the Glory Word Church Compound's marina. It, the small marina, is pictured here in satellite surveillance photos," Blaine said, as he passed out copies of the photos.

"This marina maintains an ocean-going tug with an ocean-going barge that has fuel tanks to refuel the Canary. In past operations, the tug tows the fuel barge out to the Canary when it arrives on station. We suspect that this is when victims are transferred to the Canary. The next day, the yacht leaves and shuttles 'clients' to the Canary."

John and I shook our heads. "Okay Boss, hold it," I said. "If I'm reading this right, we'd have to hit the Compound, the yacht and the Canary within minutes of each other. Am I correct?"

Blaine nodded in agreement.

John said, "Sir, we don't have the resources for an operation like this. We would need sixty, seventy men, not to mention boats."

"I know," Blaine said. "You guys don't have the manpower or the equipment. That is why this needs to be a joint force operation. We will use the FBI and DEA to hit the Compound. The Coast Guard will intercept the yacht. During that interception, the clients will be arrested and the crew along with them. We insert you guys onto the yacht in their places. That allows the third group to assault the Canary."

I stood up and asked, "What third group?"

A voice behind me said, "I think that's where I come in." It was Donny "Three Wolves," call sign Psycho. Donny stepped into the conference room and said, "Doc, I'm sorry I'm late but I have the information Colonel Blaine and I discussed."

I stood up and said, "Okay, before this goes any further let's take a break. Warlord, you take everyone down to the break room and get them a drink, stay there until I call you back. Colonel, Psycho... I need a word with you."

When everyone had left, I turned on Blaine. "Sir, I've known you for a long time. You offered us a sanction. One of the conditions I demanded is that I approve the missions and I'm directly involved in the planning of them. What is Psycho doing here and why am I just finding out about it now?"

Blaine said, quietly, "Doc, I apologize if it seems I have bypassed our agreement. It was not intentional. I called Psycho to ask a question and I guess it just got out of control. I invited him and I should have told you first thing."

Psycho started to speak but I held my hand up. I nodded. "Damn right you should have. What was the question you asked Donny?"

Blaine realized he had stepped across a line he did not want to cross again. He said, "I asked him if he could put an operational team of former Navy SEALs together and have them ready to deploy in two weeks. He said yes."

I nodded. "Okay, let me make something perfectly clear so we know exactly where we stand. No one, not even you, talks to my people behind my back. No one plans strategy with my people without my knowledge. Otherwise, you can take direct control right now and I walk."

Blaine stood, looking at me for a long time; he knew I was deadly serious. Finally, Blaine said, "Doc, you're right. I stepped over the line, it was an accident and I did not intend for this to become an issue. I'm sorry and it won't happen again."

I stared at Blaine for several minutes; finally, I said, "Okay. You understand I am serious about this and I will walk if it ever happens again?"

Blaine shook my hand and said, "I do and it won't."

I called for the others to come back. Warlord walked in and handed me a Coke. "Everything okay?" he asked.

I nodded and turned to Donny Three Wolves saying, "Ya ta hay." Psycho returned the greeting and we gave each other a back slap and hug.

One night, several years ago, a friendly competition between he and I had turned rather bloody. Both of us were bleeding from breaking tiles and concrete. I turned to Three Wolves and asked, "You don't have any blood-borne diseases do you?"

Three Wolves looked at me and said, "No, at least none that I know of."

I stuck my bloody fist out and said, "Good, now's as good a time as any; want to be blood brothers?" Three Wolves smiled and stuck his bloody fist out. Bloody knuckle to bloody knuckle, our fists met and blood mixed. Three Wolves later said, "That was not the formal ceremony, but it'll do for now."

Psycho, Donny Three Wolves, is Comanche, a descendant of Quanah Parker, as are my two kids on their mother's side. Donny is also a former Navy SEAL.

"Psycho, would you brief us all on the conversation you had with Colonel Blaine?" I asked.

"Colonel Blaine called me three days ago," Psycho said. "He asked if I thought I could get an operational team of twelve to fourteen former SEALs together for a HALO drop. I said I thought I could, then began making phone calls." He turned to Blaine, "Sir, I have your team ready."

"Psycho," Blaine said, "you're making the report to Doc. He's the TAC Leader. If he decides to use the information, it will be his team."

Psycho shifted his gaze to me and began the report. "My original mission parameters were to see if I could locate enough former SEALs to create an operational team of twelve to fourteen men capable of a HALO jump, a half-mile underwater navigation, and an assault on a small freighter held by a force of approximately thirty men, armed with small arms." He stopped and looked at me; I nodded for him to continue.

"Luckily, SEALs are like Marines. You're never an EX, you are only a former. Most of these guys have maintained their physical conditioning and many are weekend jumpers. I have you an operational team that can meet those parameters. We'll need a few jumps and some practice time but we can take the boat."

I nodded and said, "Okay, we let the Bureau and DEA take the Compound and the marina. We let part of the TAC Team, along with Psycho and his former SEALs, take the Canary. That seems to leave the rest of the TAC Team and the Coast Guard to take the yacht." I stood up and walked around for a moment before asking, "Questions?"

Warlord raised his hand. "I've got a few. First of all, are we just going to pull this yacht over to the curb or what? What is going to prevent them from radioing the Canary? How do you know where the Canary will be and what the coordinates are so we can drop the SEALs?"

I turned back to the group. "Warlord has some valid questions; anyone have any answers?"

Jed said, "The only way to stop the bad guys from radioing the Canary is electronic jamming. We still have to put people on board to seize the ship. We know the service boat will go out to refuel the Canary at sea. We track the service boat and that will give us their location. They are not going to change a deep water anchorage without reason."

"One of the difficulties in considering an attack/rescue on the Canary is that it will be difficult to get to without being seen, and the same is true for the yacht we have to intercept," I told Blaine. "I'm just not comfortable with the numbers yet, even with Psycho's additional twelve to fourteen guys. They still have to get out of the water and up the sides of the ship, and do it within our timeframe."

Standing next to the plotting table, Jed pointed to the areas of interest. "If we intercept the yacht in this area, we are still in U.S. territorial waters. I'm not worried about stopping the yacht, but I am concerned about getting someone on the Canary in time for them to assume control and stop the destruction of any evidence."

"Here's how we do that," I said. "Our plan for the Louisiana location called for parasails. We can have our eight men with powered parasails takeoff from a vessel stationed in the area. That vessel will launch the flight and continue steaming ahead. The team will form up and fly toward the Canary about fifteen miles away. What about ships radar? Will it pick the team up as they approach?"

Jed said, "Sure, but the radar signature will probably be written off as a flock of seagulls."

"I still think we need to jam the radios," Warlord said.

"I agree" Jed added, "The Airborne Warning and Control System, the AWAC plane, can handle that."

"Okay, let's lay this thing out. FBI and DEA hit the Compound here," I said, pointing at the map. "Coast Guard intercepts the yacht approximately here and boards them. All passengers and crew will be taken off at that time and replaced with our guys. Psycho's former SEALs are approximately here after being dropped by HALO. They navigate to the Canary and prepare to board. Ten members of the TAC Team fly in on powered parasails and land on deck. They seize the deck and bridge."

Jed smiled and said, "If the FBI and DEA does their job right; if the Coast Guard does their job right and if we can keep the communications jammed; if the SEALs are able to HALO onto target and arrive at the ship on time; if the team using the parasails arrive at the ship on time and are able to seize control rapidly; if the weather is right; if no one gets hurt; and if the initial taking of the ship lasts no more than ten minutes—it will all work. The operative point being the word—IF. There is a hell of a lot riding on one word that only has two letters."

I agreed, "Yeah, then the next step of the operation is to clear each room below deck, rescue the victims, secure all evidence, and..." I stopped and thought for a moment; finally I said, "Oh yeah, and we need to survive."

Chapter Twenty-Nine

Kim Rhodes sat in his study; his chair behind a massive mahogany desk. Slowly, he stood and walked down to the shooting range in the basement of his house. Closing the soundproof doors behind him, he switched on the lights and circulation fans. They would draw the air out of the room, along with the smell of gunpowder and lead particles, and exhaust it after it had been filtered.

Kim walked to the gun safe and removed a Browning .22 caliber target pistol, three magazines and two boxes of target match ammo. Pegging the target, he flipped the switch that activated the motor that pulled the target to the twenty-one-foot position. With careful deliberation, he cleared his mind, slowed his breathing, set his body and extended his right hand and the gun straight above his head; then he began the routine as he had practiced.

Slowly, his arm began to drop, bringing the weapon online with the target. CRACK! A hole appeared in the ten ring, slightly to the right of center. Again, he began the ritual. CRACK! This time the hole was slightly above the first. CRACK! This time the hole appeared dead center. CRACK! CRACK! CRACK!

The last three holes appeared as one, each touching the other. Kim smiled. After the requisite 100 rounds he fired each night, he cleaned the weapon and replaced it on its pegs in the gun safe.

He took the Wakizashi from the wall, and for thirty minutes performed katas with the razor-sharp blade before wiping down the blade and returning it to its place. Then he hit the street for a one-mile run. When he returned, he showered and went to bed.

Chapter Thirty

When he and I first met, I learned Donny Three Wolves was a Comanche Indian. His father's Indian name was Ten Bears and was a Green Beret and a war chief of the Comanche nation, so it was natural that his son followed in his footsteps. Donny had enlisted into the Navy and applied to attend the Basic Underwater Demolition School, BUDS, and had gone through the most rigorous training imaginable.

At BUDS, everyone is a volunteer. All anyone has to do to stop the torture of punishing, nonstop physical activity, sleep deprivation and ongoing operations was to walk up and grab a lanyard and ring the bell. At several points during the training, everyone considers ringing the bell and going back to the room for a beer, a burger and a woman. The best don't and Donnie didn't; instead, he earned the golden Trident of a NAVY SEAL.

After his hitch, he tried his luck in the civilian world. Like many of the warrior clan, he found he didn't care for this "other world." People in his world, the "real world," the world of the special warrior, knew that they depended on each other for survival. Theirs was a brotherhood.

In the "other world," that kind of connection was difficult, if not impossible, to find. He later found the connections he had with brothers in the "real world" often disintegrated as they walked through the "other world."

Now, after many years, he was yearning for that feeling of belonging again. He got a taste of it during the first TAC Team operation in Mexico. Those feelings were like a drink of cool water on a hot summer day. He decided to try, to the very best of his ability, to recreate those feelings again. He continued these thoughts as he pulled into my drive-way.

I heard his pickup pull in my driveway and looked out the kitchen window. I stepped outside and handed Donnie a drink. "Thanks," he said, "but no thanks. No alcohol until we finish this mission. Here," he said, handing me a thick stack of folders, "I wanted to bring the histories and medical reports on everyone to you."

I nodded and said, "So, you have your men together?"

Three Wolves nodded and said, "Yes, we started the familiarization jumps yesterday at Hooks airport. We're just doing some refresher stuff and its going well. If everything continues as good as we're doing now, we'll be doing some HALOs in the Gulf next week. The men are in good shape and most have continued to do sport jumps. It will not be a big deal to get them back into shape or refresh the jump qualifications. Main thing is we have to learn to work together; we have to be a team. That takes time to build."

I asked, "What can I do to help?"

Three Wolves shook his head, "Nothing right now. This is my part of the job. Once we're a team, I would like for you and Blaine to speak to them. Right now, I don't want them distracted."

"I understand, and that's why you're running this phase. You have my complete support. When are you going to be ready for the move to Twenty-Nine Palms?"

Three Wolves thought before he said, "We're getting close but we're not quite there. By the time we get to California, we'll be ready for the operation. Our time there will be spent refining our abilities."

"You have time for supper?" I asked. "Pam made Lasagna."

Three Wolves looked at his watch and said, "If it's ready now, I have an hour before I have to head back. I'm letting the Squad Leaders run their people through the mill."

I told him that we were just sitting down to eat. Donnie followed me inside, and after hugging Pam we sat down for supper. It was a relaxed meal; Donnie filled us in on the training regiment he had developed and the background on his people. Most were about his age, in their forties, but some were older and two were younger. They had all been SEALs, but for a variety of reasons had left the service and tried the civilian world.

"Problem is," Donnie said, "most of us enjoy the jazz, that adrenalin rush we got from the special ops training and the missions we went on. It's hard to come back to a world that doesn't involve those types of activities. It is hard to enjoy a life that doesn't have some risk in it."

I said, "Yeah, David Blaine always says, 'If you're not living on the edge, you're taking up too much room.'"

Donnie nodded, "Exactly my point. For most of these guys, me included, this operation is a God send. It will remind us of what we are, not what we were; and it just might save a life or two. It will definitely save some souls. Not a bad deal at all."

"Any problems?" I asked.

Donnie laughed. "Oh, there was a couple to start with. As always, each team will have its joker. This team's prankster drives everyone else nuts with his games, his name is George Victor. It took a day or two for him to settle down; good guy, just has an overly developed sense of the hilarious. Only other issue is a couple of guys are having some territorial disputes. You know how Alpha Males are; always trying to see who can piss higher up the tree."

"How did you solve that one?" I asked.

Donnie shoved a forkful of lasagna in his mouth and chewed. After a minute he smiled and said, "Made each one a squad leader. Gave them their own tree to piss on; things have been quiet ever since." He looked at his watch and turned to Pam. "Sweetheart, this was wonderful. I'm sorry I can't stay to help clean up but I have to get back to the troops."

Pam smiled sweetly and said, "Donnie, you're lying about wanting to help clean up but I appreciate the sentiment. I'm glad you liked the meal but I looked at your duty schedule a minute ago; you don't have anything until tomorrow at 10:00 A.M., so drag your butt in the kitchen; you're on KP."

Donnie sat there for a minute and then grinned. "Well, it was worth a try. Did you almost buy it?"

Pam shook her head and said, "No, not for a minute. How long have I known you?"

Donnie surrendered and helped clear the table. After his "chores" were completed, he hugged Pam and said he was headed to the training area. I walked out to the driveway with him. Donnie said, "Glad we could talk a minute alone. You said you wanted ten people to make up the flying squad you call the Night Hawks. My team of former SEALs will consist of twelve to fourteen people. Can we field enough extras to make this work?"

"The Coast Guard will put its own people on the yacht, so we're looking at a strike force of about twenty-two to twenty-four shooters."

"How many active dossiers have you got?"

"A total of eighteen," I said. "I have to spend some time sorting the right people to the right missions. I should have a better idea by the time I finish tonight. I need some additional troops and I don't want to just supplement the numbers by bringing in people from the Coast Guard. They have to have an understanding of how the team works or it could be a mess."

Donnie nodded and left.

Chapter Thirty-One

I went back to the War Room and picked up the dossiers again. This mission was substantially different than the last one had been. Other units would be involved, more people would be involved, and timing would be much more critical. I started with the "Night Hawks." From the ten men capable of flying the parasails, I shortened the list to eight men divided into two four-man assault teams:

Blue Team	Red Team
1. Warlord	1. Doc
2. Mighty Mouse	2. Dogman
3. Jarhead	3. Yankee Clipper
4. Squirrel	4. PIMA

I also wanted some additional fire power. I figured I'd put my two biggest men, Mountain Man and Thor, on board the yacht when it was seized by the Coast Guard. Mountain Man would bring a SAW, his Squad Automatic Weapon.

Thor would have the big surprise; he'd deliver high intensity, a half-inch hell-fire. That would come out of the mouth of the Printess .50-caliber semi-automatic rifle, designed by Robert Printess, a gunsmith from Conroe, Texas.

This weapon made its debut in the second sequel to a movie about a cyborg cop, but that had been the movies and this was going to be reality. In simple terms, Printess' toy would be able to destroy almost any obstacle with a single .50 BMG round.

The Printess .50, with a weight of 26 pounds, was not a weapon you'd want to carry while running a mile; but for this operation, it was ideal. Fitted with a static mount, scope, and 5-round magazine, it was an awesome weapon that could do magical things to an enemy. Thor was an excellent shot and with a little training by Printess, he would be able to deliver destruction to any target with precision.

I had met Thor when he was on active duty with the Air Force Hospital at Barksdale AFB. His real name was Rand Leslie. We had been reintroduced by Jim Townsend, call sign Dogman. Dogman and I worked together for several years in the Air Force Reserve Medical Squadron they were assigned to. I had started out as the First Sergeant and Dogman was the Senior Air Reserve Technician. Dogman ran the squadron during the month as a full timer.

Dogman later became the first sergeant when I left and Thor was hired to replace him. Dogman vouched for Thor and that was good enough for me. Thor was a big man, self-described as "6 feet, 2 inches tall and 242 pounds sopping wet." Dogman would replace Mongo who was out of action, and Thor would fall into Bush Hog's place since Bush Hog wouldn't be able to participate on this mission.

I also would be inserting Gregg Paul, call sign the Rev. The Rev would have his Stoner, and like with the mission to Mexico, he'd again be the primary sniper. Where Mountain Man and Thor would deliver destruction, the Rev would be more surgical with his fire power.

Psycho had total responsibility of the HALO jump and coordination of his SEALs. The plan called for me and the Night Hawks to seize control of the deck and provide cover for the SEALs to board. Once we hooked up, the real mission would start. Mountain Man and Thor would provide heavy weapons coverage top side, while two teams would go below to rescue the innocent and capture the ship.

I knew aerial fire power during the assault was essential and I had David Dillon, call sign Cobra Innkeeper, in that slot. Plus, I knew at the end of the mission, it would be critical to have a medical evacuation capability; and Cobra Innkeeper could provide that for the injured while everyone else was transported by the Coast Guard.

During the initial phone call to the Innkeeper, I discussed the operation in broad details. His main concerns were the available space and the possibility of severely wounded patients. His concern was the same as mine; if someone was seriously injured, we couldn't take too long to get them to a medical facility. He reasoned, however, that if those injured were loaded on the chopper, it would be a short flight to the mainland.

I explained that I believed twenty minutes from takeoff at the AO, Area of Operation, to touchdown on the mainland, would greatly enhance the survival potential of an injured person.

Innkeeper, a former helicopter combat pilot from the Vietnam era, asked one question. "Do you know how long it takes for someone to bleed out?"

I did but said nothing.

"Well, I do and it can take a damned sight less than twenty minutes," he said, acidly. "Well, we'll just have to do our best. Hopefully, no one will be in that bad a shape."

I looked over the dossiers of the Night Hawk team again. These eight men would have to fly in unnoticed, carrying all their gear. They would have to land unobtrusively, take control of the bridge, establish over watch security for the SEALs, and prepare to assault below deck. Dogman, the Yankee Clipper, Mighty Mouse and PIMA were new to the TAC Team, although they were not new to me; at least each was a shooter.

Dogman knew more about combat medical readiness than anyone I knew. He was rock solid and totally dependable. Moreover, he was smart, almost intuitive. He could see past the immediate into the potential and, as with any operation that went into harm's way, the ability to anticipate what your enemy might do was almost as important as what he was doing.

Thor was as big as Mountain Man. Solid at six feet, two inches, he still had speed as well as strength.

Mighty Mouse's computer and electrical expertise might just be invaluable on this mission. Yankee Clipper was smart and haunted by his past. While he hadn't mentioned it, I think he was looking at this as a chance to "square up with the universe." He and PIMA had put some the ghosts to bed—finally. The others had already proven themselves in the last operation.

My two strongest were Warlord and Psycho. Psycho was tough— he was dangerous, ergo the name Psycho—and he was absolutely confident in his training and abilities. Above all else, he was loyal and trustworthy. He would die to protect a brother.

Warlord was a tactician and he was tough and a shooter. Unconsciously I started whistling. It was an old Jodie call, a song soldiers sing when they march. "Here we go again…"

Pam walked into the War Room and over to my desk and asked, "How's it looking Hon?"

"Angel, I'm having a bit of a problem," I said, setting the beer down.

"What kind of problem?"

"When we encountered Val Richards in Mexico, we had a hell of a lot of evidence," I began. "Right now everything we have is circumstantial or testimonial. I wish we had something a little more tangible before we go in."

"Well," Pam admitted, "I can certainly understand that, but remember the circumstances are different here."

"I know, but I just don't feel good about the mission yet. What we need is Intel. Hard, indisputable intelligence that shows these sons of bitches are really sons of bitches."

"Look Baby, if you're not comfortable with this—don't go. It's as simple as that. You're the one that will be leading the mission."

"I know these bastards are dirty," I said. "But I don't want to *know* it; I want to *prove* it."

"What else is wrong?" she asked. "You've been grouchy as hell the last two days!"

"I'll tell you what the problem is; John and I have been over the numbers a dozen times. We simply cannot put enough people in the right places at the right times to ensure success. It will help that the Coast Guard can put folks on the yacht, but that's after the yacht has been stopped. We need someone on the yacht as it is being stopped to establish control and keep things from going bad; and to keep the Coast Guard personnel from taking rounds."

"Honey, I've been thinking," Pam said, slowly. "I want to do more in this operation. Last time, I couldn't really be involved. Why don't you figure a way for me to be on the inside? That way I can help you."

"I have been thinking about something very much like that," I said. "I am just not comfortable with the numbers yet. We really need people in a more flexible position."

"So what's your idea?"

"I'm not ready to say, let me play with things for a while, okay?"

"Okay, but keep me posted," Pam said.

Later, I made three phone calls; the first was to Dr. B.J. Garrett, call sign Top Eye.

Chapter Thirty-Two

"Hello Dr. Garret," I said.

"Hello yourself," Garrett replied. "What can I do for you?"

"Such a deal I have for you, Sir," I said with a smile.

"Uh-oh," Garrett said, "I don't think I'm going to like this."

"Actually Sir, I believe you will. We have another mission and I need you again." Last time, B.J. had been stuck in the position of commanding the M.A.S.H. unit. He was really disappointed about not being able to be more actively involved.

"When can you brief me?"

We made an appointment and I hung up. The second call had been to Sheriff A.J. O'Malley, I got his number from Blaine. I explained my idea to O'Malley. O'Malley had been silent for a moment then he said, "I'll make the call, if he doesn't want to go, I'll be happy to take his place." I asked him to call me the minute he had an answer.

Next, I called my daughter, Madison. When she answered, I explained my plan, what would be involved, and asked if she wanted to take part. After a minute or two, she said, "I think I can do that Dad," and began asking questions. Fifteen minutes later, she had all of her questions asked and answered. "Let's do it," she said.

Madison has always been comfortable with guns and was a great shot. In fact, until her brother joined the military, she could outshoot him with a pistol. She was strong-minded, independent and always up for a challenge. She had studied karate, SCUBA diving and knew how to rappel.

*****

The next morning B.J. and I met at a construction site not far from Garrett's office. I briefed Garrett on the information we had and how we had come up with it.

"How can I help?" Garrett asked.

"Well, I need you more involved this time," I said, and Garrett's eyes fairly lit up.

"I'm going in?" Garrett asked, excitedly.

"Well, kind of," I said, and laid out the plan. Garrett liked it, he was in.

As I drove home, I called Pam to tell her about my idea. "I want to send a unit in undercover to provide a recon of the area and gather intelligence before the assault is made. If all goes well, this will add four more people that could recon the Compound. That team will have to be on the yacht when it's seized; it depends on one guy, and I don't know if he's in yet."

Ten minutes later, O'Malley called and said, "Cochran's in. What now?"

"Tell him to get to Houston as soon as he can, that means not later than tomorrow," I said. O'Malley said he'd pass the message and to expect Cochran.

Now, I just had to figure out how to arm the undercover unit. I walked to the gun safe, spun the combination lock and looked at my options. There were not many. I figured the Compound would have metal detectors and x-ray machines at the entrances; no one would be allowed to just walk in with a weapon.

That meant I had to figure out how to get weapons on the inside. I knew getting weapons past the machines was impossible, so I'd need to focus on getting them past the people who ran the machines.

Chapter Thirty-Three

North of Houston and east of Interstate-45 is a gun shop where the grizzled genius, Robert Printess, works. I contacted him with some special requests and guidance.

Two days later, Ben Cochran, Madison, Pam and B.J. were seated when I entered my living room. Jed and Godfather were standing next to a white board, which diagramed the Compound's floor plan as they knew it from documents obtained from the County Commissioner's construction records.

"I recognize that some changes normally occur between the plans and the final product," I said. "But I'm fairly confident that if there have been changes, they are few and only minor in nature. But we need to confirm that, and the only way to do it is from the inside of the Compound."

I told them, "Your mission is to infiltrate and to verify what we think we know about the Church Compound's floor plan, confirm that it is being used for what we think it is, and lastly, to be in position to assist once the assault starts. You will literally be climbing into the snake pit."

I didn't go into the entire operation with B.J., Cochran, Madison and Pam. Should something unexpected happen, it was essential that they hold as close to their cover story as possible. Additionally, if they had too much knowledge and things went south, someone else could get hurt.

Their potential for success would be measured in their abilities to play specific parts that I had developed for each of them. If they played their parts correctly, the soft underbelly of the objective would be made available to them. Access to the Compound, the yacht and the ship, the Canary, could only be gained by invitation, guile or by force.

"If we use force too early, someone will die," I said. "Guile is sometimes as effective as a gun. B.J., you're about to become the Reverend Dr. Billy Jack Gaston," I said, with a flourish.

"Reverend Gaston is the head of a new movement in northwest Texas whose teachings are very similar to the Glory Word's. This fact will become known to the Reverend Henry Mire through articles that Dave Blaine has arranged to be published in several California area newspapers and through video articles being broadcast on television stations serving that part of the state.

"Pam, you will be the Reverend Dr. Gaston's press secretary, Pamela French. Madison, you will be the good Reverend's spiritual advisor and executive assistant, Madison McConaughey. Mr. Cochran, you will be the money behind the movement. Your job is to say little, look bored and aloof, but be ready to respond to any threat my people experience.

"B.J., your primary job is to get the ladies inside. Pam, your job is to verify the intelligence we have and pull the plug on the operation if you see something that is outside of our abilities to deal with. As a group, your job is to recon the area and gather as much intelligence as you can.

"Madison, your job will be to plant electronic gear that we can use to monitor and disrupt the Compound's communications." I slid a folded note to B.J., it simply said, "Keep your eye on Cochran, short leash." He read the note and nodded to me.

"Here is how it should work." I outlined the plan in detail. "With any luck, Reverend Henry Mire is learning about the Reverend Dr. Gaston even as we speak. I have arranged for one of our undercover governmental contacts to pass information to Mire's organization. Hopefully, Mire will identify with the similarities and want to establish contact with a like-minded brother. If not, then Reverend Dr. Gaston will simply have to make direct contact with Mire. Pamela French accompanies Reverend Dr. Gaston always. B.J., it's rumored you are having an affair with Ms. French. Hopefully, this will allow you to occasionally drift off to secluded areas and out of the way places within the resort."

B.J. and Pam nodded with understanding as I continued, "In reality, I want Mire to figure out that French is the real brains behind the movement. I want him to determine Gaston is simply a talking head that spouts the diatribe that French gives him."

I turned to the others. "Madison, you and Mr. Cochran are extra eyes and ears. Your primary function is to provide back up, distraction and assistance to B.J. and Pam. I want you two to focus on ensuring that no one is ever by themselves during this operation. Girls, if one of you goes to the bathroom, both of you go to the bathroom. Guys, you have to figure it out for yourselves, but I don't want anyone isolated from the team; agreed?" Everyone nodded.

Chapter Thirty-Four

The doorbell rang and I went to answer it. I returned with a man in blue jeans and a sports shirt. His hair, what little there was, and full beard were snow white. "Ladies and Gentlemen, I'd like to introduce Robert Printess." Printess sat down the cases he carried and shook everyone's hand.

B.J. asked, "How did you guys meet?"

Printess said, with a grin, "Doc is a gun enthusiast and I'm a gun maker. That is the start of a good relationship."

"This guy is an innovative genius with a vision to see the invisible —that allows him to do the impossible," I said. "Robert has become the team's specialty armorer."

"Well," Printess said, as he opened the two cases, "let me show you what I have come up with for your covert weapons. Madison's Palm Pilot, which is totally functional in all normal modes, will also provide a direct link to the command and control element. Real time information will be exchanged in a secure, encrypted mode that will be impossible to detect without someone having the specific frequency of transmission. Additionally, should a random search hit on the correct frequency, it will sound like static without the proper unscrambling encryption."

Printess continued, "I am particularly proud of the last two modifications; the Palm Pilot has been rigged to discharge a 60,000-volt electrical charge through electrodes concealed within a flip cover. Concealed at the other end is a single TASER unit.

"Once the protective cover is removed, two darts can be fired from the unit. Powered by a special charge, these darts trail thin copper wires and are also capable of transmitting 60,000 volts to the victim. Within fifteen feet, the darts could penetrate any clothing other than heavy leather jackets or other bulky clothes."

"And that won't be a problem," I said. "The folks who might be the recipients of the twin darts won't be wearing heavy clothing in southern California."

"That's a good thing," Printess said. Smiling, he added, "Did you know the TASER's inventor got the idea from the old Tom Swift books he had read as a child? It is a little known fact that TASER actually stands for Thomas A. Swift Electric Rifle."

"Really, I didn't know that," Madison said as she looked around at the others, obvious it was new information for them too.

"Now, for B.J.," said Printess, "I've decided the Reverend Gaston needs to walk with a limp and has to have assistance from his walking cane. That cane will actually be a modified rifle with a rotational chamber capable of firing two .357 magnum rounds before reloading. The barrel opening is covered with a rubber cap that can be fired through, if firing the weapon becomes necessary.

"Pamela French will carry a purse especially made for her. On one side, there's a large, metal buckle guaranteed to set off the metal detector. If a security check required that the purse be opened and emptied, the metal detector would still go off because of the buckle. But since the purse is obviously empty, they'll say, 'Thank you ma'am, you may proceed.'

"In fact, a North American Arms .32 caliber semi-auto will be concealed within the purse, hidden from view and, due to special padding, indiscernible to touch. The gun is loaded with seven Glassier rounds. These are devastating high expansion, low penetration rounds designed for maximum transfer of energy and the creation of massive wound channels.

"Ben Cochran will carry a day planner that has his cell phone, a mini-cassette recorder and Palm Pilot inside. The back cover, sealed with Velcro, can be pulled apart. Inside is another North American Arms semi-auto, but this one is a .380. Same scenario as Ms. French's purse, we are not trying to beat the detectors—just the people running them." He pulled out an elegant black belt with a heavy buckle. "Ben, I made this belt for you; Doc had estimated you to have a thirty-eight inch waist. Is that about right?"

"Right on the mark."

Printess nodded. "Your belt comes with a knife made by Jeff Knox of St. Louis. While it is similar to the Bowen buckle knife, this one can be drawn without losing your pants. With a subtle, decorative buckle, it is less noticeable or detectable to the average looker. You simply pull the belt out of your belt loops and lay it on the table, if you do have to go through a metal detector.

"Unless they catch it, which I doubt, put it back on and you have a three and half-inch, semi-curved, single edge blade that is partially serrated." Printess demonstrated the release; a simple snap.

Cochran put the belt on and drew the knife from its disguised sheath several times. "This is pretty handy," he said, nodding his approval. Once the items and their modifications were explained to the members of the Infiltration team, they spent time learning the specific handling characteristics of their new weapon systems.

Robert Printess was thorough and patient. Finally, he asked, "Are there any other questions?" There were none.

Each person knew that they might be required to use the weapons they had been given to defend themselves or someone else. That was the name of this game, and God help the opposition if direct action by this squad was required. Top Eye was itching to be involved, as was Madison. I had some concerns about Cochran, however.

Could he hold it together? Would he feel it necessary to avenge his daughter's pain? I didn't know and wouldn't until the operation started, but I had Top Eye there to watch him. If the other agencies did their job, if the universe smiled on us... Well again, IF can be a very big word.

"Please review the folders I have given each of you and let's discuss any questions," I said. There were none.

Jed had one comment. "I think we need to go ahead and make the aerial recon we talked about. I want to actually eyeball this place."

I nodded. "Been thinking the same thing. Godfather told me earlier this morning that he was set to make an orientation flight. Would you like to accompany him?"

"Yeah, I want to see the Compound, the marina and the surrounding area from the air," Jed said as he pulled his cell phone out of his pocket. "Let me give Godfather a call and brief him," he said as he walked outside.

"Okay," Godfather told Jed. "Why don't we take a flyby; the plane is fueled and ready to go. Let me give David Blaine a call and make sure we have a place to crash. Oops, bad choice of words. Let me make sure he can put us up for a couple of nights."

"That works for me," Jed said.

Godfather called Blaine in Palm Springs. "Sure," Blaine said, "Come on. While you're here, there are some things I need to show you and this would be a good time to do it. Do you have your own plane or are you flying commercial?"

"We'll have our own plane," Godfather said. "I'll set flight plans to the Palm Springs Airport then we can make whatever changes you want to additional flight plans."

"Good, I'll have everything set up when you get here. In fact, it would probably be a good idea to start thinking about moving everyone out here to stage for the mission."

"Doc's already working on that. We'll see you tomorrow," Godfather said, as he hung up the phone.

Chapter Thirty-Five

Two days later, David Blaine, Godfather, Jed and I were on a conference call. I said, "I think it's time that we start making the move to California. Things are going to start moving pretty fast now that we have some real-time Intel on the marina and the Glory Word Church Compound. I want our people all in the same place at the same time, ready to move."

"I agree," Blaine said. "How do you want to handle this?"

"Psycho and his SEALs can fly out tomorrow," Jed said. "David, they will need to be armed by your folks out there. The Infiltration team can fly commercially with their specialty weapons in checked baggage. The Night Hawks could fly commercially but will need clearance for their weapons, and same on weapons for those folks who will be intercepting the yacht and boarding."

"I have an idea," Godfather said. "The power packs and kites will be delivered; why don't I fly back to California with the weapons in my plane? That way we keep a low profile, and no one is the wiser."

"I like that idea," Blaine said. "Can you get all of this in the plane you're flying?"

Godfather nodded. "The personal weapons for the Night Hawks, plus the Printess .50, and the other weapons from the Interception team, should not add more than the weight of another person, maybe two. I had Jed with me on the way down, and he won't be with me on this trip, so weight shouldn't be an issue. Worst case scenario, I take on less fuel and have to add a fuel stop. It is doable."

"Alright, make that happen," I said. "I want you in the air this evening. We are getting short on time. I'll have the teams pack their weapons and weigh them for you before lunch. Will that give you enough time?"

"Sure will," Godfather replied.

"David," I said. "Can you coordinate putting everyone up in quarters, rent us some ground transportation and get air tickets for everyone?"

"Not a problem," Blaine stated. "After this call, shoot me and email with everyone's name and specific requirements. I'll take care of it."

"Boss, I've got that information," Jed said, "I'll get it to you. Plus I'll send the list of weapons, that way we don't have to add ammo to Godfather's flight considerations."

"Okay Gentlemen," I said. "We are on a tight timeline. If anything, this will give us an extra day or two for recon, training and rest. Let's get started."

I terminated the call and contacted Psycho, Rev and Warlord. My instructions were the same to each. "You and your squad pack your weapons in their cases, include all magazines and combat knives, but no ammo. Call the weights in within the hour."

I told them the harnesses, uniforms and other gear should be packed in equipment bags and checked as baggage on the commercial flight. Ammo, again, would be supplied by Blaine when the team reassembled in California.

By mid-afternoon, tickets were confirmed for everyone; quarters and four rental vans plus a car were confirmed. Godfather was already airborne and en route back to California.

That afternoon, Warlord, Psycho and I, along with our individual teams, boarded three separate flights from Houston's Bush International Airport headed for Palm Springs. The next morning at 1000 hours, we would gather all of the team members together for a planning session in Palm Springs, California.

David Blaine, who was also a real estate manager, arranged for the entire group, excepting Psycho's SEALs, to be put up in a gated mansion about twenty minutes from the Church Compound. The SEALs were, at their request, billeted at Twenty-Nine Palms Marine Base. They would drive down in two vans for the meeting.

Blaine met all three planes and coordinated the transportation and directions for each group. By 2130 hours, everyone had reached their billets, unpacked and had supper. Showers and sleep followed.

Chapter Thirty-Six

The next day, the two vans containing the SEALs arrived at the meeting location in Palm Springs. The gated mansion was massive and Blaine had even hired a staff to look after the needs of the team members. Even so, it was lucky the mass gathering would be a one-time happening. The mansion's gymnasium was the only place big enough to fit everyone. Following the meetings, the teams would split up and each element would begin its final preparations for the assault. That assault was set for five days later.

Jed began with the initial Intel brief. "Ladies and gentlemen, three days ago, Godfather and I made two flybys of the target area; one from east to west and on the return leg, west to east. Based on those flybys, we have finalized the plans. This should be the last time all of the TAC Team components will meet prior to the final assault. I assume each of the squad leaders have reviewed their operational instructions?" He received nods from around the table. "Good, then let's begin the briefing."

Over the next hour and fifteen minutes, the plan was discussed and described from each individual squad's point of view. Phase one of the operation would be an infiltration of the Compound by B.J., Pam, Ben Cochran and Madison. The information they gathered would be invaluable to the FBI and DEA squads that would descend the next day on the Compound.

Their secondary goals were to place electronic monitoring equipment in predetermined locations, and to position themselves to be on the yacht when it went out to meet the Canary.

Psycho's SEAL team would head to Twenty-Nine Palms for several days of practice jumps under the supervision of some special force parachutists with experience in this kind of warfare.

My men would be practicing the tricky elements of their specific duties. I looked at the TAC Team and said, "It has been decided the Night Hawk group will takeoff from a ship that will pass approximately three miles from the Canary and fly over water to the ship. The flight route will carry them over the open ocean.

"If anything happens in the early stages of the flight, there is a very real danger that someone will have to set down at sea. Now the good news is, we'll have a recovery craft standing by. The bad news is they can't launch a recovery attempt until the operation has been engaged.

"Additionally, anyone who has to abort will be lost to the assault team. There will be no way to rescue or recover that person in time to participate in the assault. That means if something occurs and we lose a person, number one, the assault team will have to operate short a person; there are no replacements available. Number two, the downed person will be on his own and will have to wait to be picked up by the rescue boat. Number three, if the individual were injured, this could be a serious situation.

"For this reason, each flyer will wear an inflatable life jacket, with a survival pack and a strobe beacon. The kite and the power back will both be fitted with quick release tabs so they can be ditched and not pull the flyer underwater. Fortunately, each person on the Insertion Team has received 'self-aid and buddy care' training in the military."

I continued, "If a disabled flyer had to ditch and that person could land unharmed or not so seriously injured as to be incapacitated, it would not be too unpleasant an experience. If however, the person is seriously injured, there is no way for us to get to him except by boat, after the assault is completed. That could mean a couple of hours.

"Each member of the team will be wearing a Casio Pathfinder GPS watch, model PAT 2GP1V. Water resistant to 160 feet, each watch can hold up to eight way points. The watch face displays in graphics or numeric readouts. It supplies longitude, latitude and speed calculations. Should someone have to ditch, a location will be taken by the GPS.

"If the injured flyer must hunker down," I said, "that means bobbing around in the ocean with his strobe, waiting for pickup. The Coast Guard will already be committed and in position to intercept the yacht inside U.S. territorial waters. The yacht will be ordered to heave to and prepare to be boarded. At that time, if everything goes according to plan, our Infiltration team will be in position to prevent problems which could come from the crew or passengers of the yacht."

Lynn Rogers raised his hand at the end of the briefing. "Go ahead, Mountain Man," I said.

Rogers raised himself to his full 6 foot, 2 inches, 275 pounds; he spoke softly, at least as softly as the big man could speak. "Sounds to me like you guys have really thought this thing out. Also sounds to me like this operation just needs one more thing."

"What's that?" Jed asked.

Mountain Man leaned over onto the plotting table, looked over the layout, turned and spit tobacco into the coffee can at his feet. He wiped his chin and said, seriously, "One shit-pot load of luck."

Jed nodded and said, "You're right Mountain Man, but the good news is we have surprise on our side. With a touch of luck, we'll be in an out and rescue the victims in short order."

The big man spit again into the can. "Oh, I'm up for it Jed. I just want everyone to understand this ain't gonna be a picnic."

*****

After the meeting, I talked to David Blaine. Blaine said, "Fellas, this is a pretty aggressive plan. I've got some good news and some good news. Which do you want first?"

"Well, how about the good news?"

Blaine said, "Well, looks like the Marines have a massive exercise scheduled but they can divert a Blackhawk for the rescue end of this operation. The other good news is that as of about thirty minutes ago, the recovery center is ready to be activated at Twenty-Nine Palms. What do you think?"

"Sounds good to me Boss," I said. "Psycho, how is the training going for your men?"

Donnie Three Wolves stood up. "We've finished the ground school and made orientation jumps, both daytime and nighttime. Tomorrow, we take our first HALO. We'll do two daylight jumps and one nighttime jump, all of these will be over land. If these are successful, day after tomorrow, we hit the water for the first time. We have simulated targets set up outside of the AO but with similar visual landmarks and flight time. It should be as close to the actual target requirements as we can fake."

"Good, are there any other reports?" I asked.

Chapter Thirty-Seven

The morning of the next day, the eight members of the Night Hawks team were out in an open field just north and west of Palm Springs, California. The field belonged to a friend of David Blaine who was a crop duster. There was a single-wing duster in the open hanger next to the main building. No one else was there this weekend.

Laid out on the grass were nine separate bundles, eight of us stood next to them. Next to the last stood the instructor, Mike Robinette, complete with flight suit and sunglasses. He was a big man, dark with both a hint of humor and a hint of hardness. "Good morning gentlemen, my name is Mike Robinette and I'll be your instructor and trainer."

We learned the contraption has several names: powered parasail, miniplane, paramotor or paraglider. To me it looked like someone's bad idea that had become a reality. Mighty Mouse asked, "What the hell is a powered paraglider exactly?"

Robinette said, "Nothing more than a backpack-style aircraft. It consists of a paraglider wing combined with a paramotor. The engine is used to gain or maintain altitude so the pilot can fly off level ground without the assistance of wind or thermals, like regular paragliding. The engine can then be switched off to glide or soar as desired and restarted in flight when required to gain altitude.

"A little history before we begin," he said. "1979 saw the first use of a Paramotor; ten years later, a Pagojet was offered to the public. It used a 3-cylinder engine and a mouth throttle where biting down increased power. A mercury switch in the throttle would shut off the motor when the pilot dropped the mouth piece."

He continued, "A successful foot launch from level ground was made, but the guy kept it secret until the machine he used became the first commercially viable paramotor. In 1991, the first paramotor was brought to the U.S.; since then, it has gained solid footing as a sport. Powered paragliders can be safely flown on most calm weather days. There's even some models with frames and wheels."

Dogman asked, "So, what can you do with one of these?"

"You can climb thousands of feet in the air or skim inches off the ground with them. In fact, many pilots stay between 500 and 1,000 feet above the ground. A large field clear of obstructions is plenty of room for you to land and takeoff from. The scenery is spectacular, and it is the best sense of freedom with your legs dangling from the harness. You can fly for about two to three hours at a speed of between twenty-five and thirty miles per hour on one tank of gas. By applying the brake, the paraglider can be slowed to a fast walking pace for landing."

Jarhead asked, "How fast do they fly?"

"Speed varies with the type of paraglider used, but will usually average between twenty-three and a little over forty miles per hour. This is a special model, we estimate just under forty miles per hour in these conditions."

Jarhead raised his hand again. "How long can we stay in the air on a tank of gas?"

"Motor-on flight time can easily exceed two to three hours, based upon mild throttle usage and the size of your gas tank. Periods of extended full throttle will burn fuel at a faster rate. Motor-off time is limited only by the thermals and abilities of the pilot."

"How high do they go?" Warlord asked.

"Most of the time they are flown between 500 to 2,000 feet," Mike said. "However, it will continue to climb until the thrust of the paramotor stops."

"What about takeoff?" Yankee Clipper asked.

"Nothing to it. You can takeoff almost anywhere, as long as conditions are right and you are taking off into wind and you're going to fly in good conditions. There are two ways to launch: the forward and the reverse. On the forward launch, the wing is behind you. During low or no wind conditions, you must run while pulling the wing forward, using your foot speed to inflate the wing. On the reverse launch, for slightly higher wind conditions, the pilot faces the wing, using the wind to inflate and lift the wing."

"What is the maximum wind speed a paramotor can fly in?" Yankee Clipper inquired.

"There's no problem up to ten kilometers. The upper limit of wind speed for takeoff is around twenty kilometers. Keep in mind that with twenty kilometer wind on the ground, the wind speed could be thirty to forty kilometers at altitude, and it may not then be possible to penetrate forwards, only to go backwards over the ground. That sucks!

"In these conditions, it is much more advisable not to fly, and it is often worth reminding yourself of the old aviation proverb: IT IS BETTER TO BE ON THE GROUND WISHING YOU WERE IN THE AIR, THAN TO BE IN THE AIR WISHING YOU WERE ON THE GROUND." Everyone nodded in agreement.

"What's the weight?" Squirrel asked.

"These are about sixty pounds but it can go up to around ninety for the larger units. Engine size, electric start, reserve parachute and fuel determine the true weight. You can add around eight pounds for every five liters of fuel to your overall weight," Mike told him.

Chapter Thirty-Eight

For several more minutes, Mike continued answering the team's questions. I chimed in. "What's the fuel?"

"Nothing special," Mike said, holding up a gas tank. "We'll be using premium regular gas but since the engine is a two stroke, we mix it with oil."

"What happens if the motor quits running?" I could see the question on the faces of at least two others.

Mike smiled. "Nothing! That's what makes powered paragliding so safe! Most normal landings are accomplished with the engine intentionally turned off. If the motor unexpectedly quits running, the pilot flies the paraglider normally and glides down to earth for a routine landing. You'll need good boots with ankle support. You'll probably have to run aggressively for at least ten or twelve strides on the landings we're going to do here."

"So you can restart the paramotor during flight?" I confirmed.

He nodded. "Yup, most new engines come with very high-output ignition systems. With just a small tug on the pull starter, restarting is simple. Or, even easier are the new electric starter setups. This way you can turn the engine off and soar like an eagle. Then at your discretion, restart the engine and resume flight."

"What are we going to do today?" Mighty Mouse asked.

Mike passed out a training schedule to each of us. "We'll start out with the basics of flight, some ground handling, getting the paraglider in the air, and simulated launch runs from flat ground."

Dogman raised his hand. "We dressed right? Do we need anything special?"

Mike shook his head. "No, what you're wearing is fine. Comfortable pants, good boots and a long sleeve t-shirt are what we recommend for training. Tomorrow, you should bring a long sleeve jacket and gloves, sunscreen, hat and sunglasses. You will need plenty of liquids, so be sure to bring something to carry water. The most important item is a good pair of boots. Strong ankle support, like good hiking boots that lace up over the ankle, is a must. The most common injury in powered paragliding is a sprained ankle."

I thought for a minute before asking, "How different is this canopy from a skydiving parachute?"

"They're both similar in construction to a modern, steerable ram air skydiving canopy, but different in several important ways. A paraglider is a foot-launched wing without the 'terminal velocity deployment' of a parachute. Consequently, a paraglider is designed to have a descent rate of about three feet per second, while a parachute descends at nine to eighteen feet per second; and is made much heavier to survive the loads of opening. A paraglider also has a more elongated, rectangular or elliptical shape than a parachute, and with more cells which increases its gliding performance."

"How is it different from paragliding?" I asked.

"Paragliders are usually flown without engines, from hills or mountains. The paraglider pilot needs to find rising air or lift in the form of warmer air rising in 'thermals,' or ridge-lift, where the wind is deflected upward by mountain slopes to keep flying. Finding and using lift to stay aloft is known as soaring.

"Without this lift," Mike explained, "a paraglider will gradually descend until reaching the ground. Combining a paraglider with an engine forms a powered paraglider which can be flown from level ground, without the need for hills, mountains, a winch, wind or thermals. The engine is used to gain or maintain height, and the pilot can cover vast distances without the assistance of wind or thermals. The engine can then be switched off to glide or soar as desired and restarted in flight, depending on the model, when required to gain altitude."

Mighty Mouse asked, "How do we control it?"

"The pilot pulls down on the appropriate left or right brake line that is connected to the back end of the wing with his or her hands. Pull left to go left and pull right to go right. To gain altitude, increase the power output of the paramotor with the hand throttle. To lose altitude, let up on the throttle; that reduces the thrust."

Warlord queried, "How noisy are they?"

"With the special mufflers and ear plugs, you'll have no problem. Remember, when you're at altitude with the engine off, a person on the ground won't be able to hear them. Now, let's get started."

We pulled out pocket notebooks and started making notes.

"Part one," Robinette began, "consists of the harness, backpack, propeller, propeller cage and motor. Part two, is the sail or paraglider itself. The engine is a small four-stroke," he continued.

"Built with modern technology, it's more reliable and weighs less than the older engines. The increase in performance of modern para-gliders makes it possible to fly with almost half the power of only a few years ago. It also means less vibration, the engine is easier to start, and it uses less fuel. Less weight means the pilot can run easier, faster, more erect and under better control, since he's not struggling with a heavy load."

Chapter Thirty-Nine

After we had identified the parts and pieces, Mike assembled one unit. "Like I said, to launch it... to get airborne, you lay out the sail, start the motor to fill the sail and then you takeoff running," he said, with a rueful smile.

"Question, please," the Dogman said, with his hand up. "Just how many people does it take to launch one of these things?"

"After today, each of you will be able to lay out the canopy, check your lines, attach the motor, inflate the sail and takeoff by yourselves. Really, it's not a problem. They are fun to fly and easy to learn to fly. I promise that each of you will be flying your machine comfortably by the end of the day."

Picking up each piece as he called its name, Mike said, "Now, take the harness, backpack motors, flight decks and speed bars out of your bundles and move to the hanger. Let's begin your ground school."

Over the next several hours, we learned about the machines, which the TAC Team took to calling kites. The lightweight frame was made of aluminum alloy and glass fiber, the best balance between weight and strength. The case disassembled and reassembled easily for convenient transportation.

A protective cage surrounded the propeller; and since the propeller did not turn at idle, a simpler and lighter cage was possible. The large diameter propeller meant more efficiency and less noise because the propeller turns slower. With two blades instead of three or four, it is much easier to transport.

The harness had a new system that eliminated both high and low connections. We learned that this stabilized the kite, suppressed the gyroscopic effect of the motor and let you fly "actively." This harness also provided greater safety in mishaps and a stable position during takeoff, flight and landing. It was simple, adjustable and made for a comfortable, relaxed flight.

Robinette explained, "The gas tank is transparent which allows the pilot to keep track of fuel consumption. The engine is even equipped with its own cooling fan since the body of the pilot keeps the airflow from hitting the engine directly and cooling it effectively. The engine is capable of being stopped and restarted in the air. It is fitted with a throttle control and can be operated even while wearing gloves.

"The throttle control has a safety factor, in that it is impossible to push the throttle control by accident. The diaphragm-type carburetor allows the engine to work in any position. Fuel will not be spilled during flight or transport. Competition rigs can be fitted with a basin carburetor, and suction uses even less fuel and is optimized for that kind of performance. There is even an extra tank for long range and a reserve chute that could be deployed in mid-air.

"With this setup," Robinette continued, "it is possible to paraglide in areas where fly sites or conditions are limited or nonexistent. With thorough training, a backpack motor pilot can use the motor to launch and then spend the rest of the flight 'ridge soaring' or thermaling, using the motor only when necessary to keep from landing. Paragliders differ from parachutes in that they are designed to go up instead of down.

"A front-mount flight deck, or instrument panel, is mounted on the rig and angled to allow you to view the various gauges and compass you'll need. The radio is mounted in the helmet."

By mid-afternoon, the team learned more about powered paragliders than any had thought possible. Now, it was time to launch the kites. One at a time, each man powered up the engines, filled his kite and stepped up into the heavens. The only phrase that came to my mind was, *This is a hoot!"*

*****

I had both parasailed and parachuted; this was something similar yet entirely different. It was the simplest and most serene way to fulfill man's oldest dream—free flight. Paragliding is about finesse and serenity, not strength and adrenaline. While we got to solo the first day of instruction, we still needed several days of practice.

Our kites were specially made of ripstop nylon and colored black for night operations. In our black BDUs, black boots, black balaclavas, black gloves and black helmets, we would be virtually invisible during the night operation. Landing was tricky. Robinette had told us highly ranked flyers could land on a Frisbee; we weren't that technically astute.

This was going to be where we spent the most time practicing. We had to get the landing down tight. Our flights after the first day weren't long at all. We'd go up a few hundred feet and start setting up the landings. Warlord and I, since we were going to be the first to land, totaled up many extra flights in the daylight trying to perfect our landing.

We had to "stick" the landing and be ready to catch the others as they landed, after all... our target was smaller than our level of training could get us to in the time we had. We had to learn how to flare, dumping air from the canopy and stalling, to be able to land with a minimum number of steps or we would go over the side and the mission would fail.

Each man would wear body armor, load bearing equipment, night vision goggles, a tactical radio, primary and secondary weapons plus a variety of specialized munitions and tools. What we needed was good weather—no wind or at least wind blowing in the correct direction and a moonless night.

After becoming comfortable with the flight characteristics, we moved to night operations and flights. By the third day, I was convinced I could fly the course day or night. For that matter, I was about half sure I could do it in my sleep. Landing the kites was more difficult and yet easier than we initially anticipated; it was a matter of technique. Warlord and I were perfecting the flare technique every flight.

The challenge of landing without making a commotion that would alert the crew of the Canary, was dropping significantly.

We had to land on the top of the bridge of the Canary without alerting the command center. It was going to be difficult; difficult but not impossible. It just required practice and timing. So we practiced take-offs, powered and non-powered flight and landings.

We all practiced landings on a scale model of the ship's bridge complete with radio antennae and radar booms. Warlord and I put duct tape down to reduce the size of our target by two thirds. To say the training was intense doesn't come close to describing it.

"Dressed in black, flying in the dark," I said to myself, "We really are the Night Hawks!"

Chapter Forty
D-Day minus 5 days

That same morning, Psycho was meeting with his SEAL team on the tarmac at the field at Twenty-Nine Palms Naval Air Station. There was very little conversation, which was normal for this group. They were working together but had not coalesced into a team yet. The team concept was particularly ingrained into the SEAL construct for operation.

During SEAL training, almost every person had looked longingly at the lanyard; a few individuals even did ring the bell. At that instant, their torture stopped. At that instant, they learned something both about themselves and about the men who remained.

All of the people on Psycho's team had "been there and done that," but none had ever rung the bell. Part of that was because they would not have been able to live with themselves if they had. Part of it was because they would never have been able to look another man in the eyes, had they rung the bell.

Now, they were a group of hard men who had done hard things and survived and were about to do it again. While none discussed it, all felt an excitement that they were about to prove they still had "IT." Yes, they were older. Yes, for some, their lives had not turned out exactly the way they had each envisioned, but they still had "IT" and they were about to prove it—again.

The two squad leaders who Psycho picked approached him on the tarmac. The taller of the two used the call sign Dagger while the shorter used the call sign Shadow. Dagger spoke first, "Hey, Boss. Everything has been checked out and both squads are ready to go."

Psycho nodded. "Any problems I need to know about with equipment?"

Shadow chuckled, "Naw, everything is fine. Some of the older guys needed a little more familiarization with the new stuff, but they picked right up on it and I'm comfortable with where everyone's at. They're just ready to get the 'high work' started."

Psycho motioned with his head and he, Shadow, and Dagger walked away from the main body of the team. Psycho asked, "Everybody have their head wrapped around this mission?"

Dagger spoke, "I think so. You know each of us at some point in time thought about coming back into the teams, but for whatever reason it just didn't happen. All of these guys have or had families, jobs, you know normal lives, and I think that we've carried those responsibilities as well as we could. This, however, is a chance to be who we really are, at least for a few hours or a few days. This is an important mission, but it is an important opportunity for each of us to regain 'ourselves.' You know what I mean?"

Psycho said, "I know exactly what you mean. When Doc called me for the first mission, I had the exact same thoughts. I'm glad you guys are having this opportunity. I know what it did for me."

Shadow asked, "So, are we on schedule?"

Psycho field stripped his cigarette and stowed the filter in his cargo pocket. "Yes," he said, "my primary concern is that we don't get anyone hurt in practice. We can't afford to lose any folks before the actual op. We are right on the short end of the mission now."

"You worry about the planning," Dagger said. "Shadow and I will ensure that we have everyone trained, ready and healthy."

Psycho nodded and they went back to the staging area to buckle on their equipment. Dagger, as the senior member of the team, was the jumpmaster for the training missions. He gathered everyone around him for the final briefing.

"Okay," he said. "Listen up! We have about thirty minutes before we launch so if you have to piss, get it done now. I want everybody standing in line ready to board the plane in fifteen minutes. While you are in line, I want a final equipment check; buddy up and make sure everyone is good to go. Any questions?" There were none.

Forty-five minutes later, the team was loaded and the plane was tax-iing down the runway. Inside, the two squads set on opposite sides of the plane. The seats they sat in were made of one-inch tubular webbing, woven into a loose pattern and supported by a long, aluminum pole and periodic straps attached to the wall of the plane. They weren't particularly comfortable, but no one was thinking about comfort at the moment.

The plane climbed to altitude, a process that took several minutes. Inside, the red light went on and Dagger gave the sign for his people to go on oxygen. Once the oxygen bottles were turned on and each mask was in place, the men stood and faced the rear of the plane. A final equipment check was done and each man stood ready.

The jumpmaster signaled the load master who pressed an intercom button to speak to the pilot. The load master signaled to Dagger who acknowledged the signal as the rear ramp of the plane began to lower. As soon as the seal was broken, noise and a blast of cold wind filled the plane.

Dagger stood with both arms up and watching the signal light. As soon as it turned green, Dagger dropped his arms and both lines of men ran toward the rear of the plane and launched themselves into space.

There was an instant of buffeting then a moment of disorientation until their training took over. Within seconds of exiting the plane and falling into space, the individual squad members located their team-mates and were flying in a precision formation.

They adjusted the distance between each man and between each team. It was essential that they dropped through the subarctic temperatures of high altitude and not lose track of their target on the ground.

Additionally, they must position themselves so that when the chutes were opened, they would not interfere with the opening of any other members of the team. In seconds, each man was falling at terminal velocity and his eyes were focused on his gauges. One showed how much oxygen was remaining in his bottle and the other indicated altitude.

"Now THIS is what I'm talkin' about," was the single thought that went through the mind of each man, as he fell toward earth at a rate of speed of 160 to 180 miles per hour. While there were no shouts of glee heard over the hush of wind and the mask covering each face, Psycho recognized the grin that stretched across each of the faces falling through space with him.

Psycho also knew that speeds of over 200 miles per hour were attainable in sport jumps, but that required significant practice to achieve. Besides, it's necessary to slow back down to around 110 miles per hour before opening the parachute and, even at that speed, the jolt was jarring.

Watching his dials, he saw he had dropped past the point where oxygen was needed. Now, he saw the target and focused on his point of landing. He did not stare at the target; rather he flipped his attention back and forth from the target to his altimeter. He knew that if he watched the target, there would be a tendency to forget to pull his rip cord. Many sports jumpers suffered from that mistake. Rarely did one survive.

Psycho readied himself mentally to deploy his chute. When his indicator showed 1,000 feet, he pulled the rip cord and the chute deployed. Quickly, he checked his lines and canopy and looked for the other jumpers. Everyone was exactly where he should be. They were "flying squares." The rectangular-shaped, chute canopies were incredibly maneuverable, and with 1,000 feet of altitude each man would be able to drop to pinpoint, accurate landings—which they did.

Picking the spot they wanted to land on, each man flared his chute and landed standing up. They quickly gathered their canopies and shucked helmets, masks and harnesses. There was a round of high fives and back slapping. They had ridden the dragon and survived—again.

Psycho let the revelry go on for a few minutes, it was the beginning of their team mentality. After a short while he called their attention back to business. "Alright, that was okay for the first HALO in quite a while. However, it's going to have to be a lot tighter for the operation and the opening will have to be at less than 600 feet. Let's move into the classroom and debrief."

Dagger and Shadow fell in behind the group as it headed to the small trailer that was used as a classroom for this operation. Dagger said, "Boss, I thought it went pretty well, but you seem dissatisfied. What's the matter?"

"I thought it went well also, but these guys don't need their ego stroked," Psycho said. "They need their performance enhanced and the best way to do that is to let them push themselves to places where good isn't good enough. They did great, but they can do better and they know it. I'm going to let them show me how good they can do it."

"Okay, I got you now. I'm tracking with you."

"This ain't brain surgery," Psycho said. "We know these guys have been good in the past. They want to know if they're good now. Let them push themselves; our job is to make sure they don't get hurt or over confident. You need to remember, it's only when you see a mosquito landing on your testicles that you realize there is always a way to solve problems without using violence."

Without another word, they mounted the wooden steps that led up to the trailer and went inside.

Chapter Forty-One

The Night Hawks and the SEALs continued to fly and jump for the next several days and nights. Throughout the time my men and I were in the air, Mike Robinette was in our ears. From the ground, he watched our flights and gave instructions through the radios embedded in our helmets.

We started to practice landing first with two people simultaneously and silently. That didn't work; there was not enough room on the roof of the bridge.

Then there was the problem of what to do with the kites and power packs. Just before touching down, the flyer would pull down hard on the toggles that controlled the kite. This allowed him to gently and quietly set down.

Warlord figured if at that moment the flyer hit his quick release tabs, the kite would simply drift overboard in the dark. It was tricky, but the concept was sound and after the third day, we were able to do it consistently without injury or damage to the equipment.

By the third day, the rest of the team had learned to make their landings effectively, provided Warlord and I were there to catch them. The focus shifted to the night landing; on the first try, Dogman miscalculated and slammed into Thor. Although both saw stars, neither was injured and, more importantly, neither cried out upon impact. Had this been an actual landing, they would not have alerted the bad guys.

*****

D-Day minus 3 days, 0235 hours

The barrel of the Street Sweeper came up. I saw the blast flare out of the barrel and felt the full load of 00-buckshot as it slammed into my chest, directly over my heart. It felt like a 4 X 4 fence post had hit me at about 60 miles an hour. I hit the ground on my back, ten feet from where I had started. I saw the moon come out from behind a cloud. I couldn't speak, I couldn't breathe, I couldn't move, and I couldn't see. My last thought was, "Death is not so bad; at least I don't hurt."

I awoke with a start; my body was cold with sweat. My hands were clenched and my chest hurt. This was the fifth time since this operation started that the damned dream had come back. I muttered to myself, "God, it is hell reliving your own death over and over again." The dream never got better. It was never easier to see. It was never easier to experience, and it always hurt. Each time it was simply real.

"I am getting too old for this shit," I said, aloud, stood up and headed to the bathroom. "I am getting entirely too old for this shit."

Chapter Forty-Two

Blaine was going over the numbers when a call came in on his cell; the number showed as "restricted." "Morning Colonel," the voice said, and Blaine sat upright in his chair.

"Good morning, General," Blaine said.

"I understand the operation is pulling together."

Blaine picked up a pen and fresh sheet of notebook paper to take notes. This was the person who had offered the sanction to the TAC Team. "Yes sir, it is; in fact, I'm going over the final planning right now."

"When do you think it will launch?"

"If we can coordinate the different agencies, it shouldn't be longer than forty-eight hours," Blaine said. "I was going to call you after I worked the numbers one last time."

"Any issues I need to be aware of?"

"No Sir, like last time this should be a nice, quiet, unobtrusive maneuver. In fact, we have built into it a camouflage screen that will keep the TAC Team in the shadows."

"Good David, we need to keep them in the shadows. As you know, the current administration is not known for strong positions on anything controversial."

"I understand; that should not be an issue."

"Good. We have an election coming up and things right now are somewhat..." he hesitated. "Somewhat tenuous, shall we say." The General seemed somewhat subdued.

"We still have your support, don't we Sir?" Blaine asked, with a decree of concern.

"Absolutely, but as always... caution and secrecy are the bywords."

Blaine nodded to himself. "Certainly Sir, we understand that."

"With the world situation—the increasing threat of terrorist activity, and the fact that this administration is reluctant, at best, to deal with those issues publically... Any news coverage could derail the entire operation."

"I understand Sir. As usual this is an Eyes Only project. Will you give me till this afternoon and let me call you back with the details?"

"Certainly, Colonel, I'll be looking for your call." With that the connection was broken, and Blaine set the phone receiver back in its cradle. Of all the duties he had been a part of on active duty, this was by far the most sensitive.

*****

General David C. Johnston, retired, was in Blaine's opinion the perfect American patriot. Tough and dedicated, Johnston had served as the Air Force Chief of Staff and Chairmen of the Joint Chiefs of Staff, a body of senior uniformed leaders in the Department of Defense that advise the Secretary of Defense, the National Security Council and the President on military matters. As one of the longest serving members, he had been Vice Chairman for three years and Chairman for almost four years, almost completing two full tours.

Johnston had graduated flight school, received his pilot wings and was a commissioned second lieutenant in the Army Air Forces. He served in World War II and Korea, logging over 300 hours of combat missions there; later he also served in Vietnam.

Capping a career that had included operational and command positions in bomber, tanker, training and tactical fighter units, as well as headquarters staff positions, Johnston became Chief of Staff of the Air Force.

One of Blaine's more serious official contacts with him took place about three years later when an airman at Blytheville AFB had taken a hostage. A Security Police Investigator with martial arts experience had volunteered to go in unarmed and act as an unarmed hostage exchange.

"Sir, if need be, I can take him out with my hands and feet," the investigator had told Blaine. Blaine, as the Security Police Commander, had up-channeled the report and discussed the situation with General Johnston who blessed the attempt.

The situation was resolved without gunfire. During the after action report, Blaine explained to Johnston, "The hostage taker had been up over twenty-four hours. After the exchange was made and the hostage safe, my Investigator asked him, 'Hey, do you want a beer?' The perp asked, 'Can I have one?' 'Sure,' the Investigator said, and he had two six packs delivered to the scene. After an hour and a half and several beers later, the hostage taker was emotionally deescalated and physically exhausted. He passed out drunk, and my guy just threw him over his shoulder and walked out. We took him to jail without any problem."

"Who was the Investigator? Johnston asked. He kept a pretty cool head."

"Young Staff Sergeant named Marvin Roberts," Blaine explained. "But everyone calls him Doc."

During his second tour as Chairman, Johnston worked to change the position from that of a "corporate" executive, to being recognized as the principal military advisor to the President and the Secretary of Defense. He argued the changes would improve the quality and timeliness of military advice and improve readiness and effectiveness of the combat forces.

Jones continued his efforts toward that goal after his retirement as Chairman of the Joint Chief of Staff, and saw it come to fruition with the reorganization in the mid-1980s.

By the time the Mexican operation started, Johnston, now retired, was serving as a special advisor to the National Security Council. His duties were described as "unofficial" or "unrecognized" but he was still one of the most influential men in D.C. When he scanned the initial Intel report, he thought he recognized a name and called Blaine. "David, is this guy the same one you had at Blytheville on that hostage deal?"

"Sure is Sir, same one."

"Good," was all Johnston said. At the end of that successful operation, Johnston had offered Blaine a "sanction" for the TAC Team and the rest, as they say, is history; a history that would remain secretly locked up in the National Security Council Archives and would not be released to the public for years.

Chapter Forty-Three
D-Day minus 2 days

After the third exercise of the final day I was pleased, but did not let up on the Night Hawks. Although they didn't fly again, they stripped and repacked the equipment twice more before I gave them the rest of the day off. We would leave for the rally point at 0700 the next day. Once our kites and gear were secured, it would stay that way until the launch.

I gathered the Night Hawks together after the gear was stored. "Okay," I said, "I want everyone back here at 2000 hours this evening. That means everyone, the rest of the entire team. Warlord, I want you to call B.J. and our lead sniper, Gregg Paul. Make sure everyone will be here by 1800; including Cobra Innkeeper and Nightengale. Now, go to your rooms; shit, shower and shave then get your butts back here."

Dogman asked, "What is the uniform of the day?"

"Civvies," I said. "Get moving."

*****

Before 2000 hours, they had formed up outside of the hanger and were waiting for me. Warlord saw the green Dodge Dakota cross the tarmac and head toward the hanger. "Here he comes."

I stepped out of the truck. I also had shit, showered and shaved and wore clean jeans and a fresh denim shirt. I gestured to the passenger side and said, "Someone grab the pizza and one of you help me with the rest of the rest of the food." At that moment, more vehicles began moving toward the hanger.

Top Eye, Pam, Madison and Ben Cochran got out of the first vehicle. Everyone moved to the hanger door. Inside, someone had set up
two long tables; the first one had all of the table settings, we stacked the
food on the second one. Soft drinks, pizza, a bowl of tossed salad, beer
and two bottles of Black Label Jack Daniels were set out for everyone
to serve themselves.

About that time, Psycho and his team of SEALs pulled up. Psycho
introduced them to the other members of the team. This was the only
time the entire group would be together until the op was over. I quieted
everyone down and said, "This is our last night together for a while and
I want it to be a good one."

Once everyone was settled down and seated, I asked Top Eye to
bless the meal. B.J. stood and asked, "Would you join me in a moment
of prayer?" Everyone bowed their heads. Pam and I held hands under
the table.

"Dear Lord, we ask Your blessing on this food and those about to
partake of it. We meet tonight to celebrate our friendship and to enjoy
the company of each other. Soon, we will embark on a difficult and
dangerous course and we ask You to watch out for each of us as we go
into harm's way on a worthy mission.

"We ask You to watch our families and guide our hands, and our
hearts, as we walk through a valley of darkness. We ask You to protect
us from that evil and, if it is Your will, allow us to return home after
serving your purposes as we believe You have shown us the way. In
Jesus' name, AMEN."

As one, the group echoed "Amen." I stood and said, "Thanks B.J.,
we appreciate it. Now dig in and enjoy. LET'S EAT!"

"Okay!" someone shouted.

"Hoo ah!" Jarhead joined in.

"You got it!" the Godfather added.

Music sprang into being from a jukebox in the corner of the hanger. It was the Eagles playing and spontaneously everyone was singing "I was driving down the road trying to loosen my load, I got seven women on my mind…" For the next two hours, the party waxed and waned.

For a while, it would be beer and pizza and laughter with loud music; then it just evolved to slow dancing with soft music. Our emotions jerked and jolted. At one moment everyone would be laughing and joking, and the next minute things were quiet and solemn.

For those with spouses and significant others, these were the moments of slow dancing, tight hugs and long looks. For those whose partners were not present, it was a time for sitting in the corner in tight groups, flipping through billfolds to show pictures of the family.

Warlord and Blaine were on their second round of pictures. "Sarah is five going on fifteen," John said. They both laughed. "It's good to see you again Dave, but something has been bothering me. In my memory you always seemed taller."

"Well, when you were ten years old," Blain said, "I was taller." They laughed and went back to looking at their pictures.

Jim Townsend, call sign Dogman, was in the corner on his cell phone. When I approached, he was just hanging up. "How's everyone?" I asked.

"Kathy and the kids are fine," he smiled. "Mom and Dad are still on the road to Ohio to see Mom's sister." Townsend's face was serious. His mom was a kidney patient and right now she was going through one of the difficult times.

His dad, a retired Air Force First Sergeant, was just an older version of Dogman. He looked and acted gruff and could be hard as steel; but when it came to his family, especially his mother… well, it hurt his heart to see her hurt.

Pam came up and pushed me out of the way and grabbed Townsend's arm. In a sultry voice tinged with laughter, she said, "Come on big boy—dance me around this saloon." Townsend looked at me and winked. He turned back to Pam and in a fair imitation of the "Duke" said, "Well now, little sister, I think I can oblige you. Better hang on!" He grabbed her and they spun off across the hanger floor. Soon they were dancing to Carly Simon's "*My Romance*."

When that song ended, I unplugged the jukebox and everyone took his or her seats again. "Okay folks, tomorrow will be a long day for all of us. Any last minute problems we need to address?" There were none.

"Good," I said, "then let's get a good night's sleep and meet here in the morning at 0600." Everyone nodded and there was a round of handshakes and hugs. In fifteen minutes, the hanger was empty except for Pam and me. I plugged the jukebox back in, punched some buttons then held my hand out and Pam came into my arms.

As the music started, I spun her in tight and we stepped off to Carly Simon's "*Time after Time*." It has been our song since T.K. King, call sign Wizard, and the others in my old karate class had a reception to celebrate our wedding, after the fact. George had sung the song and accompanied himself on a guitar. Pam and I loved T.K., but had to admit Carly did a better job on the song.

Not a word was said, and when the song ended, I waltzed her through the office door. "The party's not quite over," I whispered in her ear and closed the door behind us.

Chapter Forty-Four
D-Day minus 30 hours

The Night Hawks' battle packs, weapons, kites and harnesses were packed in a shipping container that had been loaded onto the large commercial fishing trawler; it would serve to take them to the area. 2nd Chance had overseen the packing and would ensure everything was secured on the fishing trawler.

Rich Leonard, call sign 2nd Chance, was part of the Blue Feather Foundation. This not-for-profit corporation had been set up after the last mission to care for the traumatized victims who had been rescued. Rich was also a heart patient.

A few years ago, an infection had all but destroyed his heart. Pam and I had gone to see him in the hospital; he was as close to death as anyone I had ever seen. I honestly didn't expect to see him alive again.

A few days after what I thought would be our last visit, a traffic accident in New Orleans took the life of an eighteen-year-old man. That family, in an act of incredible courage and generosity, allowed surgeons to harvest organs from their brain-dead son. Part of him lives on today and it's the reason for his call sign, 2nd Chance.

To make this trip, 2nd Chance had pushed the schedule on his next routine exam and passed it. He flew out the next day and started taking control of the team's equipment. By 0600, everyone else was there, and by 0620 the gear loading was complete. We went over individual squad assignments a last time.

I said, "B.J. and the Insertion Team will leave with us and will also be at the Hilton. They'll pay a visit to the Compound this evening. I want the Night Hawks and the SEALs to stay low-key and get rest tonight. Tomorrow, we'll have a final check of weapons and equipment."

"Cobra Innkeeper and Nightingale will be headed to Twenty-Nine Palms Naval Air Station to ensure all elements of the air support including all needed medical supplies are ready," I continued. "Timing of the assault and the arrival of all elements is critical."

Innkeeper spoke up at that point and added, "The flight from the Canary to Twenty-Nine Palms should only take about twenty minutes flying time. I think we can get anyone out in less than ten minutes, provided we don't have a lot of serious injuries and the ambulances are standing by."

"What about you, Jed?" I asked.

"I'll be monitoring communications from the Coast Guard Cutter," he said. "All units will be tied together but on different frequencies. I'll act as coordinator to make sure everyone is where they are supposed to be when they are supposed to be."

I stood up and walked to the window. Slowly, I turned around and said, "Okay, then it's a go. Good luck folks and Godspeed."

Chapter Forty-Five
D-Day minus 28 hours, Infiltration Team

B.J., Ben Cochran, Pam and Madison arrived at the Compound and pulled up to the guard shack. They were on time for the meeting between Reverends Gaston and Mire, which had been setup by the contacts. As anticipated, they were stopped and provided identification.

The fake IDs were good enough to pass any inspection. This was because they were real. David Blaine had made several phone calls and arranged for new identities with existing pictures from their real driver's licenses.

Once they passed the initial security check at the guard shack, they drove through the check point and parked in the parking lot. For a moment, the four just sat there collecting themselves. Pam broke the mood and said, "Everyone ready? Let's roll." The front two doors opened simultaneously.

Ben opened the right, rear door and B.J. stepped out looking like a southern Colonel in a bad Tennessee Williams' play. Dressed in a white, linen suit, he extended his arms and said, "Ladies" and the two dark clad women took one each. With Ben behind them, they walked to the pathway and up to the front of the Compound. It almost looked like a conventional modern resort, almost. To a trained eye the security cameras were obvious, as were the individuals standing at strategic locations on the veranda.

B.J. pushed the doorbell with his cane. A man in butlery opened the door and welcomed Reverend Billy Jack Gaston and his entourage by their names. "Please, have a seat in the sitting room; someone is on the way to escort you."

The Reverend Henry Mire arrived in about two minutes with a smile on his face and his hand out to shake that of the Reverend Gaston; two men were with him. One was Kim Rhodes, with an air of grace and expensive cologne. The other was simply muscle but there was a lot of it there. As they started to follow Reverend Henry Mire, Muscles said, in a deep and raspy voice, "Excuse me but may I see the ladies' bags? Security, you understand."

The security wand was passed over the women's bodies, as well as the Reverend Billy Jack and Ben Cochran. Once they were cleared, the cane, purse and Palm Pilot were examined and handed back without comment. Pam and Madison exchanged glances; they had made it inside and still had their weapons.

B.J. was eloquent and expansive with his praise of the facility. During their several phone conversations of the past few days, B.J. had made it clear that his predilections and those of Reverend Mire flowed along similar paths. All of these conversations were being recorded by Cochran's day planner to be used in the trials that would follow this operation.

Once Mire had determined that B.J. and he were of "like minds," he quickly and openly discussed the "advantages" of participating with the Compound's extracurricular activities.

Now, B.J. listened intently while Reverend Mire explained the intricacies of the resort's Church and library and study areas on the first floor. Then they toured the casino, lounges and restaurant, all of which were in the sub-basement area, hidden from obvious view. "Well, Reverend Mire," said B.J., with a lascivious grin. "These are lovely but what about the other 'activities' you were telling me about?"

"Why Reverend Gaston," said Reverend Mire, smiling with equal lasciviousness. "Are you sure we should be discussing such matters in front of these ladies? What about their sensibilities?"

"Reverend Mire," B.J. said, "it is exactly because of their sensibilities that I ask."

"Then let's go to the elevator. The upper floors are reserved for our more 'enlightened members.'"

Pam looked at her watch. It was now 11:45 P.M. The Reverend Henry Mire walked to the control panel for the elevator, inserted a key and turned it. The mechanism began to lower the car. Pam watched as he returned the key to a watch pocket in his vest.

Kim Rhodes and Muscles remained on the ground floor. Reverend Mire wanted to escort the little group himself. When the elevator hissed open on the second floor, B.J. took Pam's left arm and Madison extended her left arm for the Reverend Henry Mire.

Pam had positioned her purse on her right shoulder and had undone the latch that held the purse's cover. This would grant her quicker access to the .32 caliber automatic secreted there. Madison didn't have a purse but kept the Palm Pilot in her right hand.

In addition to some of its more innocuous abilities, her Palm Pilot contained digital pictures of over 100 missing persons from six parishes that had surrounded the Compound when it was still in Louisiana. They hoped it would be useful in identifying possible victims they met tonight.

Reverend Mire escorted them past several rooms in which seductively clad women and men were obviously engaging in a variety of sexual encounters. "Oh, my," Pam said, with false naïveté.

B.J. took the lead and said, "Now, now, Miss French, as I told you, we are here to sample the sweets of life and the joys of heaven."

Madison simply snuggled closer to Reverend Mire while squeezing his arm in what Mere figured was a grip of passion. Actually, Madison was trying to determine if he was armed. She didn't think so. She fingered the hidden button on her Palm Pilot and the electrodes appeared, but no one noticed.

In her sexiest voice, Madison looked up at the Reverend Mire and said, "My gracious, if this is what happens on the second floor, I can't wait to see the third floor."

"Well," Mire began, "the third floor is usually not on the tour. It is for our clients whose tastes tend to run to the extremes. It may not be suitable for you," he said, smiling.

"Reverend Mire," she said, and looked him intensely in the eyes, "you have no idea what my tastes are like." Then she licked her lips and squeezed his arm even tighter.

The Reverend Henry Mire was excited; in fact, he was almost beside himself. *This is working so well.* Mire thought, *These four will open new doors and opportunities we haven't yet strived for.*

"Well," Mire said. "If you are sure, but remember I warned you." He laughed and the three of them laughed.

"I'll certainly remember you warned us," Reverend Billy Jack Gaston said, with a smile.

"Me too," crooned Pam, and made a show of moving B.J.'s arm around her waist.

Madison squeezed Mire still tighter. Mire lead the way back to the elevator and the three of them stepped in. When the doors opened again, the view was atrocious.

The aromas of weed, sex and crack cocaine blended into a heady atmosphere that seemed surreal and reeked of sensuous abandon. Lounging in various stages of undress were four children, aged ten to fifteen years old. The Reverend Mire gestured to the Reverend Billy Jack Gaston. "My dear Sir, I hope that you and your ladies will feel free to enjoy the sweetest of the sweets. I shall return later."

"Thank you so much, Reverend," B.J. said, equally expansive. "I assure you, we shall take full advantage of the opportunity." He looked at Madison who nodded slightly and flicked a switch on the Palm Pilot. She pulled her lipstick from her pocket and made one counter clockwise turn of the cap and applied some to her lips. With the switch flipped on the modified Palm Pilot, the two devices created a disruption on all audio and video transmissions within 150 feet of the source. That source was hidden within the lipstick holder; she secreted it behind a curtain that draped to the floor.

Once Mire left, the children were afraid they were simply going to be further abused by these newcomers. But while Ben stood guard at the door, B.J. and the girls covered the kids' nakedness and moved back from them; the children realized they were there to help, not hurt.

For the next two hours, they interviewed the children confirming their identities and stories of how they had come to be there. They had been drugged and kidnapped. They had been drugged and raped. Then had been drugged and made to perform sexually while the Reverend Mire videotaped them. Then they had been made to watch the tapes, only this time they were not drugged.

The psychological rape had been even worse than the physical rape. The more B.J., Ben, Madison and Pam learned, the more resolve they had to take these sons of bitches down. At the end of two hours, the four rearranged their clothes, mussed their hair and adopted the appearance of zoned-out, sexed-out, satiated perverts.

The Reverend Mire wanted to have further discussion but B.J. was able to convince him that the "ladies" had had all they could tolerate for one night. He promised they'd be back tomorrow night to fully "sample" Mire's hospitality.

Mire said, "Why not join us for a special evening tomorrow? We're taking the yacht out and I believe I can promise you an evening you'll never forget." B.J. accepted the invitation with a smile. B.J. thought, *Yeah, and I'll promise you an evening you'll never forget.*

He nodded to Pam and the four walked outside to their Cadillac. Cochran got behind the wheel and slowly drove out of the graveled parking area. A mile away from the Compound, Madison flipped the switch on the Palm Pilot. The electronic disruption at the Compound was eliminated without any apparent connection to their visit and the "source" was still onsite—ready to be activated tomorrow when H-Hour arrived.

Cochran said, in a low voice, "These are the sons of bitches that hurt my daughter, aren't they?"

"No," B.J. said, as he leaned up from the backseat to put his hand on Cochran's shoulder. "Doc and his men destroyed the people who hurt your daughter. These are people like them that are hurting other people's children. You'll get to help these children; you'll be responsible for their salvation."

They returned to mansion where they met me and debriefed. Now, I had my proof; incontrovertible evidence of kidnapping, rape and abuse. I silently wished I did not, but I vowed to even the score for these kids who no one had tried to save. By the time the debriefing was finished, everyone was drained, including me. Later, when Pam and I were in bed and tried to sleep, tears ran down our cheeks and there was nothing we could say or do; but that would change tomorrow night.

Everyone slept late the next morning, trying to pack as much rest as they could before that night's attack. Once they were awake, each knew they would not sleep again until after the night's business had been completed. As individuals awoke, they completed their morning ritual and went down to the large dining area for breakfast.

Strangely enough, they all arrived within ten minutes of each other. They nodded to each other, but sat quietly and ate alone in their own thoughts. Each was in his own head, reviewing his own memories. When they finished breakfast, they met outside and walked around the grounds for about an hour. By the time they returned, the morning dismals were gone and they were back to business.

Chapter Forty-Six
D-Day minus 14 hours

David Blaine had arrived at Twenty-Nine Palms and established the control and communications system that would monitor all radio traffic tonight. Blaine had everything set up for the arrival of the hostages and the transfer of any injured to the local hospital where Nightingale, the team nurse, would be ready.

The SEAL team performed final checks on each person's own equipment. These checks had been performed at least fifty times over the last week, but it was a necessary part of the routine. Each weapon was disassembled, cleaned and reassembled with loving care. Although each knife was razor sharp, a final unnecessary touchup would be performed before the routine was completed.

Each pouch was emptied and refilled. Each part of the uniform was examined. Lengths of rope were undone and redone. Every cartridge was once again hand-cycled through the weapon it was designed for. It was all done in silence. Only the sound of music from the radio and the click of a cycled weapon, or the snick of a blade along an oiled whet rock or diamond sharpener, could be heard.

Then they went on to complete their final phase of preparation. "Shit, shower, shave and saddle up!" as I called it. It was a time-honored routine that actually had a purpose. Fear had a way of emptying the alimentary canal. Most folks agreed it was better to plan that part than leave it to chance. Showering was important physically as well as emotionally. The cleaner the body, the less likelihood there is of infection following injury.

It was time for the Night Hawks to leave. As they dropped their gear outside, I turned to B.J., "Top Eye."

"I know," B.J. said, "I'll take care of them," and twirled his two-shot cane gun.

"You'd better," I warned. I checked Pam's hideaway gun and gave her a hug. Then I kissed my forefinger and drew a line down the center of her forehead terminating it at the bridge of her nose. "Mark against evil," I said, ritualistically.

She pulled me close, kissed my forehead and said, "Mark of the Coonass, it'll protect you. Be careful Baby."

"You too," I said, hugging her again. Then I turned to Madison and gave her a hug. "You two stay close to B.J. and Ben and don't take chances. Remember, when the assault begins, you hunker down and wait for it to get over. We need you for Intel and directions. I don't want you joining the fray. You are too limited on available firepower."

"We know, Dad," Madison agreed. "You guys be careful and we'll see you when this is over." She hugged me, and I pitched my gear in the back of 2nd Chance's van and climbed in.

An hour later, the Infiltration team, B.J., Ben Cochran, Madison and Pam, headed to the Cadillac. B.J. got into the back seat with the two women as Ben prepared to act as chauffeur. Reverend B.J. and Ben were both decked out in white linen suits. B.J.'s was complete with a matching Panama hat. Madison and Pam were in their "uniforms for the night." Both were in black skirts with black jackets and white open-neck blouses.

Their hairdos matched, with Pam wearing a wig, their hair was pulled tight toward the back of the head where it terminated in a bun. Both wore large horn-rimmed glasses. Cochran said, "You two look like the stereotypical, tight-assed secretary with repressed desires."

"That's the plan," Madison said, in a deep Southern accent. "Our salvation, the Reverend Billy Jack, will lead us to new levels of self-awareness and experimentation tonight."

B.J. sat between the two women in black. "I feel like the cream filled center of an Oreo cookie." The girls laughed and settled into the Caddy and headed to the Compound.

Chapter Forty-Seven
D-Day, 13 hours before H-hour

The trip to the marina, where the fishing trawler was moored, only took about twenty minutes and another fifteen minutes and the gear was loaded and secured on deck. The Night Hawks began the wait; that was the hard part. Around noon, the Night Hawks felt the engines come online and they began moving out of the harbor for their rendezvous with justice.

Across the marina, Jed climbed onto the pier where the Coast Guard Cutters were docked. He presented his identification and boarded the first of the two ships. He reported to the radio shack where a Chief Petty Officer reviewed the operational instructions on the communication setup they would be using for the operation. Twenty minutes later, the Operation Commander ordered both ships to start engines and prepare to move out.

On board the fishing trawler, the Night Hawk squad members began final preparations for a night attack. Black boots, black BDUs, black balaclavas and yellow-tinted goggles were the uniform of the day, or actually the night. Under each BDU blouse was a bullet-resistant vest with shock plates, front and rear. After the blast I had taken in Mexico, these became standard uniform parts and everyone realized their value.

Tactical shin and knee guards were placed and tactical elbow guards were added. Though lightweight, they were as uncomfortable as they looked. During an assault, one never knew what to expect or when it would be necessary to drop into a prone shooting position. Special Ops personnel knew the value of knee and elbow protection. The hard, articulated ABS plastic was padded with foam and attached by elastic bands. They were reminiscent of medieval armor.

We buckled on our black combat harnesses. These were not the H- or Y-shaped L.B.E.s of the Vietnam War. They were tactical and technical marvels that would allow each warrior to carry a variety of munitions and equipment necessary for his part of the operation.

Radios, personal medical kits, extra ammunition for primary and secondary weapons, gas masks, flashlights, repelling gear, handguns and combat blades were loaded into and onto these harnesses.

On the back was a place for a Camel Back Hydration unit and a heavy-duty, drag handle which would be used if it became necessary to drag the injured wearer. Although the contents of some pouches were left to individual taste, the location of the medical kit and ammunition was standard throughout the team. This was necessary because in a firefight, there is no time to go searching for where "Billy Bob" put his bullets. You have to be able to find it in the dark and in a hurry.

Black gloves, flight goggles and black helmets with flip-down NVGs for Warlord and me completed the rigs. Armament was left to the individual. Riding in a custom made holster were my two handguns. The holster was made by Jerry Ahern; he called it the "Frankenstein holster."

Under my left arm rode the Widow Maker, my custom .45 Para Ordnance, two 12-round magazines and a Gerber Model 1 boot knife. Under the right was the Beretta 92FS, two 15-round mags and a tactical flashlight. On my right hip rode three 30-round mags for the Berretta. On my left were two 20-round mags for the Widow Maker.

The pouches on the assault vest contained extra 30-round magazines for the Carbon 15 .223 rifle; this would be my primary weapon. Fully equipped, I viewed myself in the full-length mirror. I smirked and mumbled, "I look like Ninja meets spaceman and commando."

I took the helmet, goggles and balaclava off and placed them in a helmet bag. I met Dogman in the passage way as we headed up on deck.

Dogman carried an AR-15 with a 4X scope, see-through mounts and a 30-round magazine. On his left hip he carried a Glock model 27 .45 in a low slung SAS holster that held two extra magazines. An Al Mar Warrior Combat Knife hung from his right side and he had taped a Ka-bar to his left harness strap. Extra mags for the AR were in mag pouches on his belt.

"How you doing?" I asked.

"I'm ready." Dogman was notorious for not saying much when saying little got the message across. Together, we crossed the deck to where Warlord was checking his own gear. John had his stainless Para Ordnance .45 and extra magazines in a shoulder holster that was one of the first two of the model Jerry Ahern had made; at least that's the story we got.

His customized Model 1911 .45, also named The Warlord, loaded with a 10-round magazine and two extra mags, rode in an SAS combo holster low on his right thigh.

On his left side, he carried a Cold Steel Trail Master Bowie with a Carbon V blade. On his right side was a Cold Steel SRK; its Carbon V blade had been blackened at the factory. He carried his Bush Master .223. John touched his left breast pocket and felt his .25 caliber Pen Gun.

He and I both carried one round in the Pen Gun and six extras in a waterproof tube. He had originally doubted the sense in having such a gun initially, except that it was awfully novel. But he found that with a little practice and a two-handed grip, he could regularly hit a man-size target in the head at twenty feet. He replaced his black chromed A.G. Russell Sting into the special sheath he had sewn on his right shoulder strap.

Yankee Clipper carried a full sized, tricked out Mossberg Model 590 12-gauge with extended magazine. Once his parasail landed, he would provide external security for the Night Hawks. Strapped to his right leg and buckled to his gear harness was a cut down Winchester Model 1400 12-gauge pump, sporting a pistol grip for up close work and a tactical flashlight.

On his left hip, in a cross draw Alessi holster, was his old Colt .45 pistol. Its slab-sided design by John Browning, while almost a hundred years old, was still a standard for professional warriors. When asked why he still carried the old .45, Yankee Clipper's standard answer was, "Because they don't make a .46."

Jarhead was taping the sling and swivels on his SKS for silent movement; he just couldn't break that habit. He was comfortable with this rifle; it had been with him so long it felt like an extension of him. He didn't really aim the gun. He'd look where he wanted the bullet to go and that's where it went. As the only Marine, Jarhead still found himself the brunt of numerous attacks from the other members of the unit.

While everybody else was convinced "God made Marines for us to pick on," Jarhead was convinced "these poor devils are just jealous." So in the time honored tradition, an intense but good-natured, inter-service rivalry continued. In addition to his M-9 Berretta, he carried two Kabars. The one on his left hip was a "utility knife." The other was taped to his left shoulder strap; when he pulled this one, someone was going to die very quickly and very quietly.

David LaBorde, call sign Squirrel, had been a door gunner on Dave Dillon's Blackhawk during the TAC Team's Mexican raid. This was his first time as a ground pounder with the Team. Squirrel liked two or three weapons—the Ma Deuce .50 heavy machine gun, the M-60 and a 12-gauge pump shotgun as his primary weapon. He carried a Berretta 9mm like the pistol he was issued in the National Guard. He didn't care for knives, "Don't believe in getting' that close to someone you're gonna have to kill," he would say in his Cajun accent. He sat now going through his weapons checks, magazine checks and making sure he had alternated buck shot with slugs in the 12-guage.

*****

Across several miles of desert, a C-130 on the runaway at Twenty-Nine Palms Marine Base set with the brakes locked and the engines running. On board, Psycho sat with his team. He was armed with a Bennelli 12-gauge. It was a monster shotgun that could be fired semi or pump action at the flip of a switch. Under his parachute harness, he carried a special chest-mounted ammo pack of shotgun speed loaders; two in each of six compartments.

On his left shoulder strap, he had taped his Navy Mark II knife. He had used this knife when he was a SEAL; the edge was like a razor. On his left hip, he carried a Cold Steel Recon Tanto with blackened blade; on his right was his Sig Saur .45 loaded with Corbon ammo. He knew there would be no need to double tap when using this ammo.

He looked over his team; they were set and ready. The practice jumps had honed them to near perfection. Now it was time for the real thing. As he looked at the lined faces smeared with camo paint, he couldn't help but see these middle aged men as the warriors they used to be, or he thought, *as they still are.*

Chapter Forty-Eight
D-Day, H-Hour minus 2 hours—The Night Hawks

On deck of the fishing trawler, 2nd Chance had opened the containers and helped distribute the kites and power packs. Sails and engines were stacked out of the way on the deck of the ship. The flyers stood together, silent in their own thoughts.

I explained to the Captain what we would need in the way of support. "Basically," I began, "this is a pretty simple operation. I need your nets either taken down or switched to one side of the boat to allow my people a clear launch runway. At a specified time, I'll need you to turn into the wind long enough for us to launch. After we're gone, go back to your own business."

The Captain, a retired Navy Master Chief, said he understood and ordered his crew to begin positioning the nets and other equipment to allow for a clear launch. Thirty minutes later, the men were on deck and in uniform with everything in position for takeoff. All we had to do was put on the flight engines and connect our harnesses to the kites.

The wind was blowing slightly from the north, the sky was clear. 2nd Chance pulled a large thermos from his A Bag. He passed out Styrofoam cups and poured each flyer a cup of hot coffee. When the coffee was gone, he collected the cups.

Gloves, balaclavas, helmets and goggles were put on. 2nd Chance went to each member in turn and helped hoist the flight engine up so the member could slide on their harness. Once it was buckled on and shifted to make it comfortable, 2nd Chance connected the kite's lines and helped spread the kite out behind the flyer.

Fifteen minutes later everyone was hooked up and ready to go. I gave the signal to start engines; eight right hands found toggles and jerked downward. Eight engines sputtered to life. The motors sounded and air began filling the canopies behind each man. When everyone gave the thumbs up, I turned to 2nd Chance to wave goodbye, but 2nd Chance was not waving. He was standing at attention, holding a salute.

I motioned to the flying squad; each turned and saluted 2nd Chance, then in turn took a few running steps into the wind and were airborne. I was the last to salute and still 2nd Chance held the salute. Not until I took my running steps and became airborne did he drop the salute. Under his breath he whispered, "Be careful."

Chapter Forty-Nine
D-Day, H-Hour minus 2 hours

On the Coast Guard Cutter, Mountain Man carried the SAW over to where the Rev sat with his Stoner. Neither man said anything. Mountain Man had a 15-shot Ruger P-89 9mm on the hip opposite his Ruana Bowie knife. The Bowie had a grip in which stag inserts had been mounted in what looked like a solid polished aluminum handle. The blade was ten inches long, over two inches wide in some places, and more than a quarter-inch thick.

A solid bar of brass had been inlaid along the spine of the blade. This was something old time knife fighters from the 1800s had used. When the hardened edge of an opponent's knife would hit the soft brass, the brass would catch and hold the blade, if the defender twisted hard enough and fast enough; at least that was the theory.

Mountain Man was quiet. He sat in silence watching the ocean as it moved past the bow of the cutter and he continued to whet the blade of the Ruana on a pocket stone.

On shore, teams of DEA, ATF and FBI agents were poised and ready to hit the Compound. They arrived over two hours before the yacht was due to leave the marina. They spent the time watching and listening. The controls for the electronic jamming device Madison and Pam had planted, had been activated; and for the past two hours, randomly disrupted communications within the Compound.

For the last hour, agents had alternately turned the electronic jamming source on and off at random to establish a pattern of "trouble" that would not be associated with their arrival.

As it came closer and closer to the time of the attack, the process continued. "Disruption! Disruption corrected! Disruption again, corrected again!" The men monitoring the security monitors at the Compound were convinced that there was an electrical short somewhere. Fifteen minutes before the assault would start, the lead agent would flip the switch for the final time and let the disruption roar.

Agent Mack Bryson watched as the entourage left the main building of the Compound and headed down toward the marina. He watched Ben Cochran's right hand through the high powered binoculars set on a tripod within the mobile command post that was disguised as a RV.

"There," Bryson said, aloud. "There's the signal." He picked up the microphone and said, "It is a go, I repeat, it is a go! Let them move away from the marina and make sure the radio is jammed before we move out." He received acknowledgement from the four different ground team leaders that would be making the assault a reality.

B.J., Pam and Madison were being helped on board the yacht, the Harem Queen. Ben Cochran shook off the helping hand of a deckhand and climbed aboard. He turned and looked at the Church Compound and spit tobacco into the water next to the dock before turning back to look at Mire. Ben smiled and said, "Well, looks like it's about time, Reverend."

Mire smiled, thinking Cochran was talking about the yacht leaving. "Sure is."

Cochran smiled, and repeated in a lower tone that rang with a note of steel, "Sure is!"

The four of them, under the escort of the Reverend Henry Mire, moved to the rear deck of the yacht. As the yacht started its engines, Pam pocketed the North American Arms .32. Madison gripped the Palm Pilot more tightly, and B.J. flicked the safety of the cane gun to the "off" position. Cochran simply shifted his weight and stood rock still.

Chapter Fifty
D-Day, H-Hour minus 2 hours,
Twenty-Nine Palms Marine Base

Dave Blaine sat at the Flight Ops desk. Jean Bracken, the Nightingale, was outside the building going over the flight checklist with David Dillon, the Cobra Innkeeper. Blaine was in jeans, boots and a cowboy shirt. He knew he was stuck with desk duty tonight. He resented it, but knew there was nothing he could do about it.

As during the operation in Mexico, Jean Bracken would be responsible for medical care and Dillon for flight operations. This operation was different but their roles were pretty much the same; he's flying a chopper, she's patching wounds. Command and control of the individual aspects of this mission were essential and I knew that no one was better able to coordinate the actions than "the Boss."

Blaine was anxious, but his focus had to be on the administrative and logistical aspects of this mission. They had to gear up for the arrival and transfer of the hostages the team expected to rescue. That meant at least two area hospitals had to have teams ready to cover a mass casualty exercise.

They had to have the emergency services necessary. They had to coordinate several separate law enforcement agencies' involvement in tonight's operation, and there was just two hours before kickoff. "You know, Innkeeper," Blaine said, in a quiet voice when Dillon walked in. "It would sure be a nice night to fly."

"You are sure right there, Sir," Innkeeper said. "This mission planning and support crap would not set well with me either."

"Hoo ah, Hoo ah," Dave Blaine said. "Well, back to business. Is there anything else we need to lock in?"

"We have confirmation that the other units have already left for their particular rally points," Innkeeper said. "Doc will be contacting us on his way in. He will radio us when they have made the hit and Nightingale and I will leave at that time."

"Any idea how long after the hit you will land here?" Blaine asked.

Innkeeper looked at his wrist watch. "After the pickup, and if everything goes well, it shouldn't take but a few minutes to get back here; fifteen, twenty at the most."

Blaine looked at his watch and said, "Well, it won't be long now. It won't be long at all. Is the field ready for shutdown as I requested?"

"Yes Sir, as soon as we get a call that the chopper is inbound."

"Very good," Dave concluded.

Chapter Fifty-One
D-Day minus 90 minutes

It took about fifteen minutes for the Harem Queen to clear the harbor, and about another fifteen before the two Coast Guard Cutters announced their presence. The first realization of their presence came when sirens began whooping from two directions. Until that moment, the yacht was a fun-filled party barge with music, laughter and drugs in open use. The Captain of the yacht was ordered to reduce speed.

He picked up the radio mic and called over the marine channel, "Coast Guard Cutters, this is the pleasure yacht, Harem Queen. I have only passengers aboard; what is the reason for this stop?"

"Harem Queen, this is the Lieutenant Commander Ball. I require you to standby for boarding."

"Lieutenant Commander Ball, this is Captain Ferris of the Harem Queen, I ask again. What is the purpose of this stop and why do you wish to board my ship?"

"Captain Ferris, this is Lieutenant Commander Ball. The purpose for this stop will be explained to you upon our arrival. Now, I am ordering you to heave to and prepare to be boarded. This is your final warning." Ferris acknowledged and ordered the yacht to stop.

One cutter pulled directly in front of the Harem Queen and the other placed itself in position to provide over watch. Three inflatable Zodiac boats were launched from the nearest cutter. Two of these established over watch while the third approached the port side of the Harem Queen.

As soon as the first Zodiac came alongside the Harem Queen, five of the six people in the Zodiac climbed on board. They carried small machine guns at port arms and moved to secure the deck. The pilot of the first Zodiac pulled away to allow the second to disembark its crew, while the third moved to disembark at the stern of the boat.

At that moment, the yacht was plunged into brooding silence. Several clients looked furtively around for an escape route, but there was none. The Reverend Henry Mire made a stupid move to reach under his jacket for his fully engraved and nickel plated Walther PPK.

At that moment, Madison placed the electrode of the Palm Pilot's stungun function to the neck of the Reverend Henry Mire and discharged 60,000 volts. Mire dropped like a sledge-hammered steer.

Pam drew her .32 and Ben Cochran his .380; they provided cover as the boarding party climbed on board. B.J. secured the lower deck by standing in the hatchway with his two-shot cane gun. In under a minute, after the engines were stopped, the Harem Queen was secured and in the hands of the U.S. Coast Guard.

B.J. pulled two pair of flex cuffs from around his waist and moved first to Mire's hands and then his feet, cuffing him with the hard plastic. Once finished, B.J. stood up and retrieved his cane gun. Gripping the cane like a long-barrel pistol, B.J. slapped Mire back into unconsciousness.

Within fifteen minutes of the engine stop, the Harem Queen's passengers and crew were being loaded to one of the Coast Guard Cutters; and the yacht was in motion again to make its rendezvous with the converted freighter known as the Canary. A radio call from the Canary was expected since the Harem Queen was a few minutes over due.

The Coast Guard Master Chief piloting the boat had been especially chosen for this mission. He spoke in Tagalog, one of the primary languages of the Republic of Philippines.

The Filipino crew of the Canary was pleasantly surprised to hear a countryman. He explained the engines were performing poorly and they would be delayed, but only a few minutes. Eight minutes later, the Chief made a radio call announcing the Harem Queen was en route to the Canary.

Above deck, "passengers" were stationed and were ready to act as the yacht came closer to the Canary. Pam, Madison, Ben and B.J. would be the first "passengers" to disembark from the Haram Queen. The Canary expected to see women, and they would. Additionally, the sniper team of Mountain Man, the Rev, and Thor, along with two female Coast Guard personnel, had been stationed onboard the yacht in civilian clothes to help with the deception.

Almost twenty minutes late for the rendezvous, the Harem Queen limped and sputtered alongside the Canary. No sooner had the passengers begun to disembark when there was trouble. From below deck, a blast of light and sound erupted from the Harem Queen, followed almost immediately by smoke.

The Canary crewman who had secured the Harem Queen to the gangway quickly untied the yacht and ordered her to pull away from the Canary. He radioed the bridge, and in Tagalog requested that the Captain launch lifeboats. There was an emergency on the yacht.

Twelve individuals, seven men and five females, disembarked just before the explosion. When the explosion occurred, they were directed to run up the gangway and inside the larger ship; they complied. There they were stopped by several men who obviously worked for the Corporation. Three were white, two were black, and all wore expensive suits.

Chapter Fifty-Two
D-Day, H-Hour minus 30 minutes

Once my feet had cleared the deck of the fishing trawler, the clock began counting. The assault was underway. After taking off into the wind, the Night Hawks joined up and began a turn from a northerly path to a heading of south-by-southeast. Right before liftoff, each member had slapped the Cyalume light stick affixed to the engine cage he wore, which provided a ready reference for the airborne team.

The night was clear and calm; we were lucky—no moon. With the engines muffled, it was almost silent as we flew. The wind was steady and we climbed steadily to a height of 3,500 feet. The ocean was calm and the team was making good time.

I signaled for the team's attention then gave them the signal to prepare to activate their strobe units. When my GPS showed the correct position, I gave the signal to activate. For exactly fifteen seconds, there was a new constellation in the night sky, and then it vanished forever. I knew from experience on practice runs that at any distance, the flashes would be lost in the twinkling of the night stars.

An observer would have to be lucky or looking for the strobes to see them. Hopefully, the only people looking would be Psycho and his SEALs. When they saw the strobes, that would be the signal that the assault was about to begin. At almost the same time, two shooting stars appeared.

These shooting stars rose silently from the ocean into the sky; they were green in color. These were the prearranged signal flares Psycho's team used to acknowledge they spotted the Night Hawks and they were on station and ready. In five minutes, the two teams would arrive at the Canary.

Minutes later, I looked down and to the right—I spotted the Canary. Its anchors were out but there were lights on the Canary, which meant that at least one boiler was still in operation. The deck lights framed the bridge; it was an obvious and easy target. I got everyone's attention and pointed toward the ship.

I got an acknowledgement from each squad member then began setting up the formation for landing. At 3,500 feet, we cut our engines and began the landing glide. The Night Hawks had dropped about 1,500 feet when we passed over the Canary.

About a quarter mile down wind, we turned back into the wind and set up for the landing. The trick was to approach low enough and at the right speed, to be able to flare out, dump the air in our sails, and land standing up. Warlord and I were the first two set up to land, and I touched down first. I flared the chute, popped the quick releases and the kite flew off and into the ocean.

I hit the second quick release, pulled the parasail's engine off my back and sat it on the deck. Then I turned to help Warlord land.

Because I was already standing on what little room we had to land, we had decided to make sequential, rather than simultaneous, landings. That way the first man could assist the second. It worked. In seconds, both of us stood on top of the bridge, armed and ready to fight; the kites and engines discarded and out of the way. Yankee Clipper landed next, and took up his position and kept scanning the area for trouble with the muzzle of the 590.

I heard a whistle that announced the arrival of the next Night Hawk landing. I motioned to Warlord who swung off the roof and pointed his .45 at the bridge crew. They froze. The rest of the Night Hawks landed and stripped their gear. Dogman was last to land. He zeroed in on the center of the deck. "Couldn't have been a better landing," he said in a whisper.

Freed from the burdens of their kites and backpacks, the men pulled their weapons; locked and loaded. When everyone was ready, I signaled "Go" and entered the bridge and told the officers and men present they would not be hurt if they obeyed.

It was obvious these were just the sailors of the Canary, not the criminal element that owned and operated it; however, I directed Warlord to put the flex cuffs on their hands and duct tape their mouths.

Blue team went to the rail on the starboard side of the ship and pulled knotted ropes from around their waists, secured them to the rails and dropped the lines overboard. Then they turned and set up for covering positions. Red team went to the hatchways and stood guard over each. Warlord and I finished securing the bridge crew and joined our men. Intraship communications then went down.

By this time, Psycho and his SEALs had climbed up the ropes dropped by Blue team and were on deck and ready. The entire team was now in position to begin the raid. The alarm had not been sounded and not a shot had been fired. Warlord and Psycho stood ready. I turned to the two of them and said, "Okay, we're in position; any problems?" Warlord and Psycho looked over their shoulders at their men then turned back to me.

"No!" they said, in unison.

Nodding, I said, quietly, "Then let's end it now. Be careful and watch your asses!" The swarm of men separated into three lines of warriors, each line headed for its own date with destiny and destruction. Below decks, the Corporation's staff was preparing to welcome the Harem Queen's passengers and clients.

There were two decks that contained a total of twenty-two staterooms, a galley and two bars below the main deck. These were where 'business' was conducted.

The crew's quarters were on the third level down, and there was no contact between the crew, clients, or those unfortunates who were to become pawns of pleasure. Two decks below on the port side of the ship, those preparing to receive the Harem Queen still had no idea the ship's bridge and deck had been captured.

Chapter Fifty-Three
H-Hour, All Hell Breaks Loose

Mighty Mouse and Psycho met at the aft hatchway while the remainder of the Night Hawks secured and locked every hatchway that led below, except three; these I had covered. This was probably an unnecessary measure but I believed it was better to be safe than sorry.

I watched as the passenger yacht, Harem Queen, pulled back alongside the Canary and positioned itself next to the gangway that was lowered from the hatchway on deck two. The Corporations staff members were expecting to off-load thirty-four people from the yacht.

When about half of them were off-loaded and stumbling up the gangway, there was a scream and a flash that was followed by the sound of an explosion. Smoke began to billow out of the yacht's lower decks.

Everyone's attention had been focused on the yacht as it dropped lines and moved away from the Canary. Ostensibly, this was to protect the ship. In reality, the maneuver was to prevent the Corporation's personnel from learning, prior to the assault, that their passengers had been substituted by TAC Team members. It worked.

The "fire" on the Harem Queen was apparently quickly put out and it pulled back up to the Canary. Crewmen from the large ship stood by on the gangway with heavy fire extinguishers and anxious looks, as the ropes from the Harem Queen were caught and the yacht pulled in. With their attention focused on the yacht, the crew and hard guys were still trying to figure out what had happened to it when the first inkling of trouble made itself known.

As the passengers climbed up the gangway to the first deck, a very large man walked toward Madison; he was black and bald and not smiling. He held out his hand and said, "My name is Thomas. May I have your tickets please?" While B.J. and Cochran made a big play of reaching inside their jackets for the tickets, the others pushed forward and presented their tickets.

Madison reversed the Palm Pilot to allow discharge of the TASER cartridge. She fired the TASER into the big black man's chest and triggered the charge. Thomas was taking the full charge of the TASER. Immediately fine muscle coordination, like drawing his pistol, was out of the question. Thomas took one stumbling step before collapsing in a heap. Madison backed away from the falling giant.

The TASER was losing power; Madison had already hit the charge trigger three times. Each time she fired, the big black man twitched and dropped to the deck. But within seconds of the charge stopping, Thomas would shake his head and start trying to get up.

Cochran stepped forward, drawing the buckle knife and shoving it under the man's throat. "Move and I'll cut your throat." Thomas stopped struggling and nodded; Cochran sucker punched him with a huge, tanned left fist to the jaw. He dropped like a box of rocks.

"That ought to keep the som' bitch down," Cochran said, as he resheathed the blade. B.J. moved in and put flex cuffs on Thomas. The crewmen and the Corporation's hard men had not seen the threat in time to respond. They were still on the gangway and were hustled inside.

The four undercover members who had already boarded drew their weapons and covered the other four men and those crewmen who were helping to off-load the Harem Queen. Mountain Man, the Rev and Thor were carrying suitcases, and were accompanied by three disguised female Coast Guard members. Moving to the upper deck, they opened the suitcases and pulled out their weapons. The Rev had his pride and joy; a Stoner SR-25 .308, semi-automatic Counter Sniper Rifle, fitted with Shepherd Rangefinder 6 X 14 scope that at 100 yards gave him almost same hole accuracy. Mountain Man pulled the SAW and locked a belt of .223s in place. Thor pulled out the Printess .50 cal and locked in a 5-round magazine.

They moved toward the bridge and set up and covered the deck. Once everyone was in place, I led my Red team down the aft hatchway. Warlord led his Blue team down the bow hatchway, while the SEALs headed down the starboard hatchway. The port hatchway was left un-secured as a convenient way out for anyone that could find it; straight in a kill zone.

That hatchway was covered by the Rev and his sniper rifle. My Red team moved down the gantry toward Deck Two. Warlord's Blue team would follow in moments down via another gantry. The Night Hawks had half of the ship and Psycho's SEALs had the other. B.J.'s team re-formed, and moved forward as a group to the next internal checkpoint within the ship.

Once inside the interior of the ship, it looked like the front desk of a fine hotel. Madison had the Palm Pilot out again, and flipped the pro-tective cover back exposing the electrical terminals of the stungun func-tion, powered by its own battery.

A clerk, bell man and the concierge were on duty. She approached the concierge and breathless asked, "What's happening? That beautiful yacht appears to be sinking in front of my very eyes!"

"What are you talking about?" he asked, as he grabbed for a wall phone to call for information. Madison touched his neck with the ter-minals. He opened his mouth to speak, stiffened in shock and collapsed without dialing the connection.

Swiftly, but silently on the cushioned soles of their combat boots, Red and Blue teams came down the stairs at the end of a long hallway. Two by two, we set out down the hallway. The two high men, Squirrel and Jarhead, were covering the doors on the opposite side of the passage way. The two low men, PIMA and Yankee Clipper, focused on the path we had come down and provided rear security. When they came to the first hatch, they paused. Yankee Clipper slung the 590 over his shoulder and pulled the sawed off from his leg holster. It was time for some close up work.

The team configuration shifted. Dogman turned and covered the rear with his full attention and the AR. Warlord and Mighty Mouse prepared to enter the room, while I maintained watch over the unexplored portion of the hall. On the count of three, they entered fast and hard. I heard several of the little pops made by the suppressed Ruger .22.

Mighty Mouse came out first and changed mags in his silenced Ruger .22. Warlord came out next, moved to my side and whispered, "Two down, two hostages. I told them to stay where they were, we'd be back for them." Without taking my eyes off the hallway, I nodded.

When they were ready to advance, Warlord tapped Dogman and me twice on the shoulder. The assault teams moved further down the hall; so far we had not been discovered. The next door was on my side. Warlord and I moved into position and Mighty Mouse passed me the silenced pistol. I dropped my .223 on its tactical sling; it automatically positioned itself across my chest.

We had come to the area where the ship stopped looking like a ship. The modifications were extreme and the interior looked like a five-star hotel. Hatches were gone and now replaced by conventional doors. The harsh metal passage way was replaced by paneling, carpet and conventional lighting.

I whispered, "On three." I moved my gloved fist and held up one, two, three fingers, then eased the last door handle open. As we came to the first room, we prepared for entry.

With two people covering, Squirrel picked the lock and eased the door open. The room was dark and the green glow illuminated a victim stretched on a vertical rack. Beside the rack, there was a man and woman coupled with the wild abandon of a drug-induced sexual euphoria.

Silently, I stared at the body on the rack. I couldn't even tell if it had been male or female. The intestines had spilled out of the stomach wall, and covered the two lovers. We didn't have the luxury of being shocked or sickened by the horror of what we were looking at.

The lovers humped faster and faster, but they never made it to climax. I put two rounds in each of them. I shot the man in the buttocks and when he whirled, I gave him a third eye between the two he already had. I shot the bitch in the stomach when her partner fell off of her, then gave her a third eye too.

I said to Warlord, "I wished I could say they suffered, that was my intent, but I think he was just surprised. I don't think she even knew we were in the room."

As we stepped into the hallway, the area exploded in a blinding flash of light. In the next instant we were trapped in the light. Dogman reacted first; his shotgun roared and two flechette rounds tore into the light-bearer. The small-winged darts peppered his target's flesh, shredding it and the light like razors.

With the roar of the shotgun, the team went hard and fast to secure the hallway. Four hard asses spilled out of the two rooms at the far end of the hall. My .223 opened up and Warlord's was right beside it. A wall of tumblers blasted down the hallway and tore through the wall of hard asses. Dogman threw a flash bang grenade then suddenly he was slammed down, hard. He was hit square between the shoulder blades and was lying face down.

When I reached him and rolled him over, his eyes were fixed and distant. "Shit," I said, but at that moment Dogman's eyes flashed and he jerked up out of my hands. The next thing I knew, Dogman was standing over me with fire in his eyes and his .223 at the ready.

"Son of a bitch, that hurts," Dogman said, through clenched teeth. "It must have been a stray from one of those assholes." He pointed back toward the enemy bastards down in the passage way. "Lucky, I was wearing this vest."

Near the bow, Psycho flipped the lever on his Bennelli to semi and Dagger threw two flash bang grenades toward the hard asses that were coming at them from the room at the end of the corridor. Dagger threw another one back the way they had come.

Although stunned by the blasts, the bastards kept coming. They were firing blindly but they were firing none the less. Psycho ordered, "Take 'em!" Dagger opened up with his MP-5; 9mm slugs punched through the jackets and shirts of the gunsels.

Shadow's team was providing rear security during the fracas. When the gunfire stopped and the smoke cleared, they counted four more bad guys down; no injuries among the SEALs.

Excepting the orders given, no one spoke during the short intense battle. Quickly, security was established and teams went door to door to clear rooms, rescue victims and dispatch assholes. In less than three minutes, they cleared eight rooms, found six victims and determined that all of the assholes already lay dead in the corridor.

Psycho had the victims frisked and escorted to the upper decks under guard of men from Dagger and Shadow's squads. They then focused their attention on the next gantry that led to the deck below. Shadow turned toward his men. Once he had made eye contact with each man on his team, he nodded and moved out. He had no need to look behind him; he knew his men were behind him and moving with him.

He smiled for a moment and thought, *Feels good to be back!* Three slugs slammed into his back at that exact instant.

Chapter Fifty-Four

Red and Blue teams cleared the rest of the rooms on their end of deck two without having to exterminate any more of the vermin that had inhabited that floor. Total body count so far was six dead, five rescued, casualties—none. In combat formation, the team moved down the stairwell to the third level. At the end of the stairwell was a door. As I prepared to blow it, it swung open slowly and a rakish figure stood in the opening.

"Well come on Doc," B.J. said, "You're burnin' daylight."

I stepped around him, found Pam, kissed her quickly, gave her the Beretta and shoved her and Madison into the team's perimeter. Warlord gave Madison his Sig Pro .40. Both girls verified the chambers were loaded and took up positions. B.J. stuck his now useless cane gun through his belt and accepted a Carbon 15, a .223 caliber pistol with two 30-round magazines, joined together in what's called a "jungle clip." Cochran was handed a Smith Model 29, a silver .44 magnum with an 8 3/8 inch barrel and a full cylinder and three speed loaders, by Thor.

Now that I had found the girls, B.J. and Cochran safe, I felt a lot better. Things had gone pretty good so far. They gathered up the hostages and moved them up to the second floor, and put them in the same room as the ones rescued by B.J. and the girls. A quick check raised the body count again: eight bad guys down and/or dead, eight rescued, still no casualties. We'd been lucky, so far.

I positioned B.J.'s team to secure the room with the rescued hostages. Dogman peeled his medical pack and began treating the hostages with Madison's help. They made a good team. Pam and Top Eye covered the two ends of the hallway, while Psycho, PIMA and I prepared to take the next level.

I was prepared to take the stairwell door that exited onto the floor below, but I decided to go at things a little differently this time. Instead of jerk and jump, I decided on shoot and scoot. PIMA loaded three Door Buster rounds into his shotgun and fired. The two hinges disappeared first, followed by the doorknob.

The staccato spraying of several 9mm machine guns ripped the stairs and walls. "Glad we changed tactics," Warlord said, with a smile. I nodded and pulled two flash bang grenades from my vest and showed them to my team; they nodded. Then I pulled the pins, released the spoons and counted to three before dropping them down the stairs. The two flash bangs went off as they bounced through the door and onto the first floor.

My team was facing away from the light and their cover absorbed the shock. Warlord pitched one grenade, then a second; he and Squirrel waited. When they went off, the flash was not as bright.

These were hand grenades, designed to kill and maim, not shock and incapacitate. As Warlord and Squirrel hit the landing, one went left and one went right and they both opened up. Nothing standing survived.

Trying to escape the battle below decks, four bad guys ran up the forward ladder at the end of the passageway, straight into the cross hairs of the Rev's scope. Before they could raise their weapons, the Rev blew the two over the deck rails from the impact of center mass shots with the .308.

His third shot hit the next one in the face, and a spray of bone, brains and blood launched out of the back of his destroyed head. The fourth bad guy fired a burst and ducked behind solid steel as the rounds ricocheted. Thor shifted slightly and sent 670 grains of destruction through that bulkhead, through the last man's subgun and through his head.

Mountain Man leveled the SAW, spraying the downed men and the hatch they had come through. Six more dropped below decks just from the ricocheting .223 slugs.

Chapter Fifty-Five

Below decks, PIMA was engaged in a shootout with two guys when suddenly his assault rifle stopped functioning. Two attempts to clear the .223 by pulling the charging handle rearward had failed; the damn thing wouldn't budge. PIMA dropped the useless weapon to hang by its sling, and tore his 1911 .45 from his Alessi belt holster. The .45 ACP's well-deserved reputation for both accuracy and stopping power performed as expected.

Recognizing that PIMA's shooting had stopped, two more gunsels advanced on his position figuring to finish him off. Before they had advanced halfway down the passage way, PIMA dropped one with a shot to the knee. He put two in the chest of the other and fired again on the first. He killed him with a heart shot, just as a blast from Yankee Clipper took the man's head off.

"Sorry I'm late PIMA, got kinda hung up back here," Yankee Clipper said, with a rue smile.

PIMA smiled back, "Better late than never Clipper. Let's go." Clipper handed him the 590 shotgun to replace the jammed .223 and they were off. Rounding the corner they dropped three more bad guys without slowing their pace.

Below the decks, Shadow was slumped against the wall, unconscious. Blood covered his face and had splattered over the wall. He wasn't breathing. Dagger motioned for his squad to provide cover then knelt next to Shadow and laid him flat on the floor. With two swipes of Dagger's combat knife, Shadow's blouse and vest had been cut away.

Dagger rubbed his hands in disbelief across Shadow's unmarked t-shirt. "No blood!" Immediately, he felt for a pulse and listened for breathing. Neither was present. He sliced off the t-shirt and saw two large lacerated bruises already forming on his head. "Blunt Shock Trauma!" he said. "Start CPR while I take a look at his head." While the rest kept security, two men moved forward: one to do compressions and one to provide ventilation.

Dagger warned, "Check his ribs, they could be broken and you'll just cut him up on the inside doing compressions." The man nodded and traced the bone structure under the forming bruises.

The SEAL began pushing on Shadow's chest in a coordinated rhythm of breathes to compressions performed. From what Dagger could tell, the third bullet had dug a neat crease along the right side of Shadow's head. About then, Shadow gave a coughing lunge and tried to sit up. Dagger held him down until he could tell that Shadow was aware of where he was and what was going on.

"What the hell?" Shadow said, confused.

"You took three rounds," Dagger said. "Luckily, you had your vest on and you have a hell of a hard head." Over his shoulder Dagger instructed two men, "Move him to the rear and let's clear this floor!"

Shadow sat up and said, "No one's moving me nowhere, no how! Now what room did that son of a bitch shoot me from?"

Dagger pointed down the hall; Shadow nodded. He picked two men and said, "On me, the rest of you on security." Quickly, the three SEALs moved toward the door. With hand signals, Shadow told his people what to do. The shot gunner would blast the door hinges, Number 2 would kick the door, and Shadow would do the entry. They would initiate on three.

Shadow flipped the safety on his MP-5 and held up three fingers. He folded one down, then the next, then the last; only a fist remained. When he jerked his left fist down, the little subgun in his right hand fired two bursts in rapid succession.

There was a blur to his left as he launched himself through the door and onto the deck as a shotgun roared at him. Shadow rose up and moved to check the hard ass he'd just killed. He walked back into the hall and said, "Son of a bitch won't shoot me again."

Later Dagger would tell him, "It sounded like BOOM! BOOM! Blap! Bang! Bang! Bang!"

"Let's get back to work," Dagger said. "We're almost finished!" Less than ten minutes later, they had completed their search and rescue mission. The ship was secured and more victims were rescued.

Mountain Man, Rev and Thor had established fighting positions to cover the withdrawal. Psycho's SEALs were already dropping the lines and cables overboard. These could've interfered with the helicopter coming in to pick up the injured passengers and transport them to Twenty-Nine Palms. Debris from the battle was being pitched over-board, clearing the deck of any obstructions. The first ones out would be the most seriously injured and the Night Hawks.

The plan called for the crew of the Canary and the surviving bad guys, to be taken off on the Canary and the Harlem Queen's life boats under the guard of Coast Guard Zodiac boats that had pulled close to the gangway. They'd be picked up by one of the two Coast Guard Cutters standing by.

The uninjured victims would go via the Harem Queen back to the marina. SEALs were to be extracted by Zodiacs to other cutter. The injured and the TAC Team would be evacuated by Innkeeper's Black-hawk. As I looked up, I saw the Innkeeper's landing lights flash on; he was standing by to land. We moved out.

Squirrel went out to direct the chopper down while the Rev and Thor provided security. Mountain Man was ready to supervise the passengers movement so they could be loaded on the yacht. I watched as the Black

Hawk helicopter settled to the deck only about fifty feet from the ship's bridge.

I could see the yacht off the port side. The yacht, no longer smoking and with its engines running perfectly, was returned to the gangway. Those uninjured rescued victims were being loaded onto on the Queen as Mountain Man stood security next to the gangway. The injured were being loaded onto the chopper. On the opposite side of the ship, the crew and staff were being off-loaded into life boats by Psycho and his SEALs. A U.S. Naval Cruiser had been dispatched to pick them up.

When the uninjured victims were loaded onto the Harem Queen, Mountain Man returned to the main deck. He was standing, watching the loading of the chopper when suddenly, he dropped his rifle and collapsed. It was obvious he'd been shot but no one heard the sound of the shot over the chopper's rotor.

I waved everyone down and moved to the big, wounded man. Once I saw Mountain Man's leg, I knew there was no choice. Dogman jerked a bandana out of his pocket and pulled it tight around the wound. Then we half-dragged and half-carried the big man to the door of the chopper and pushed him in. Mighty Mouse jumped in beside him and pulled him further inside. He waved at me, indicating he would ride with the wounded man.

I knew I would not be able to load my Night Hawks onto the Blackhawk. Every minute of delay added to the potential loss of Mountain Man and certainly to the loss of his leg. I knew that in all probability the leg was going to be lost. I had one chance to save it and that was for him to be on the chopper; I waved to Innkeeper to takeoff.

Nightingale was finished working on a female victim and rushed to the side of Mountain Man. Nightingale wrapped a pressure bandage around the injured leg and began inflating it by blowing into the inlet. Rogers tapped her shoulder and she turned.

He shouted over the engine noise as the chopper lifted off, "Put a piece of surgical hose on the inlet and let me have it. You take care of the others." She nodded and stuck a piece of hose on the inlet. She then passed the other end to Rogers, who began to inflate his own pressure bandage.

She shook her head. *There's a man,* she thought. Then she reflected, *A man in the company of men.* She smiled and went to work on the hostages.

Up front, Innkeeper lifted the Blackhawk off the deck then dropped its nose in forward flight. He knew every minute counted, and that whether or not the Mountain Man kept his mangled leg depended more on his skills as a pilot than on Nightingale's skills as a nurse. Sweat was rolling off his forehead. Under his breath he kept muttering, "Come on baby, come on baby."

Innkeeper climbed to about 150 feet and pulled a slow bank to the left. He eased the yoke forward and continued to gain altitude. Gradually, he began to relax. When he was flying straight and level, he adjusted the collective and began to hum, "That's the way uh-huh uh-huh, I like it uh-huh uh-huh."

Mighty Mouse tapped Nightingales shoulder and shouted, "I'm going up front for a look see and to help Innkeeper."

"Okay, but don't take long, we'll be at Twenty-Nine Palms in just a few minutes," Nightingale ordered.

Mighty Mouse acknowledged, "Roger, give me just a minute or two to assess things and I'll be back." Nightingale checked the vitals on her two patients. When Mighty Mouse took off his headset and was no longer able to hear her, she looked at the now unconscious Rogers and muttered, "Son of a bitch!"

Chapter Fifty-Six

While the Black Hawk lifted off, I stood watching the operation. No other gunshots cut the night. I did not know where the shot that hit Mountain Man had come from or who had fired it. Psycho's SEALs had jumped to action and were scouring the ship to find the shooter. They searched rapidly and thoroughly, but in the end they found nothing. It was like the shot had come from nowhere.

I was overseeing the final stage. All of the evidence—computer hard drives, note books, video tapes—everything had been loaded on the Harem Queen for transport to the mainland. The two boxes that Godfather had picked up at Barksdale were broken out. Inside each box was ten pounds of C-4 that had been sent by Blaine.

Now that the chopper had left, the C-4 was being strategically placed by Psycho's people. The crew had been off-loaded on their life boats and life rafts, and had paddled or been towed by Coast Guard runabouts to the cutters. Psycho's SEALs were completing a final bow-to-stern sweep of all decks. They were looking for any stragglers and any additional evidence.

Thor approached and handed me the radio controlled detonator. I asked, "Everyone clear?"

"All of our people are. We still did not find the shooter. Anyone left is not going to mind the noise. Psycho's team should be finished in..." Thor looked at his watch, "another fifteen minutes."

"Move all of our people off this tub," I said. Thor nodded and soon everyone but the SEALs and TAC Team, were off-loaded into the emptied Zodiacs. Eight minutes later, the SEALs and I left the ship. It was a little cramped in the Zodiacs. Psycho and I crouched in the inflatable as the outboard was cranked and the Coast Guard Coxswain piloted the boat about 100 yards from the Canary.

I pulled two cigars and a flask out of my combat vest. "Got time for that drink now?" I asked. Donny Three Wolves took the cigar and touched a flame to it. He took off his cover and wiped his head with the towel he had around his neck. "Believe I will, thanks Doc."

I passed him the flask; on its side was an old military toast. It said, "To us and those like us—Damn few left." Donny took a swig and said, "Damn few left is right." I laughed. By the time we finished our cigars, all of the team members were aboard the cutter.

I flipped the cigar overboard and gestured toward the ship. "Shall we?" I asked.

Psycho passed the empty flask back to me and flipped his cigar over the side. "Let's do it."

I hollered, "FIRE IN THE HOLE!" and hit the charger.

The blast was incredible, even at the distance we were from the Canary. The resulting fire was quickly destroying everything. The ship started listing to starboard almost immediately as fire and smoke billowed from the charred hull. I then felt a hand touch mine; it was John. John had a small engraved flask in his outstretched hand; it was an exact duplicate of the one I carried. "As it says, Dad, 'To us and those like us.'"

"Damned few left," I finished as I took a swig and smiled at my son. I was awfully proud of the man he had become. Then my attention was pulled back to a spot in the dark. The hair on the back of my neck was standing at attention, but my continued stare saw nothing.

Finally, I shook my head and turned away and said to John, "We have a treasure trove of information of the Corporation and its illegal activities. The final body count, I think... about twenty-eight bad guys dead with a bunch wounded. Most won't survive and the ones who do will go to jail for a hell of a long time. Nineteen victims rescued, most with minor injuries. Looks like about five more seriously injured. Only two wounded on our side and they should make it."

Not a bad operation, I thought. *Not bad at all.*

Chapter Fifty-Seven
On Board the Chopper

As he crossed the coast line, Innkeeper began a clean turn to port and triggered the radio to reach the Command Section. "Boss, this is Innkeeper inbound with injured; two serious. We will need ambulances on standby, ready to move the minute the passengers are off-loaded."

"Roger, Innkeeper. Are any of the injured ours?" Blaine asked.

"Affirmative, Mountain Man took a round through his left knee, it's not life threatening and he's stabilized; but I would not want to take book on his chances of keeping that leg," Innkeeper said. Moments later he could see the base at Twenty-Nine Palms approaching below and slightly to the left.

He was about eight miles from where he knew the runway ought to be when a sequenced series of white strobes cut through the night. These strobes looked like balls of brilliant white light rolling directly to the approach end of the runway, a comforting sight indeed.

"Mighty Mouse," Innkeeper said, to the man in the co-pilot's seat. "Tell Nightingale to get Mountain Man ready to off-load. I want him in the first ambulance and I want her to stay with him. I'll meet her at the hospital after everything here has settled down."

Mighty Mouse nodded and keyed the intercom that allowed him to talk directly to Nightingale's headset. She looked up once and nodded her understanding and compliance. Pointing to two hostages, she said, "You two stay here with him and tell the rest we'll be down in less than five minutes."

Innkeeper keyed the intercom again, "Please put your seatbacks and tray tables in their full upright and locked positions. Please remain seated until the aircraft has come to a full stop and the captain has turned off the fasten seatbelt signs."

Nightingale laughed and flipped him the bird. The green threshold lights passed under the chopper and Innkeeper began setting up for landing. The big chopper descended like a giant bird; softly the wheels touched down and Innkeeper gave the controls a twist and drove along the runway, stopping just short of the first ambulance.

He hollered over his shoulder as the engines died, "Y'all move him toward the door; I want to get him on that ambulance as quick as we can." Innkeeper could see the ambulance backing toward the door.

"Let's get it open and get them on their way. You folks sitting on the floor, stay there until we get these injured unloaded and then you can carefully exit. There will be drinks, food and blankets waiting for each of you, no need to rush."

The Mountain Man, conscious again, was the first off, followed by Shadow. As they were getting him onto the gurney and tied down for the ride to the hospital, Mountain Man looked up at Innkeeper and said, "I surely do appreciate the ride and the good looking stewardess, but you gotta work on the in-flight entertainment."

Innkeeper laughed and said, "I'll take that under advisement, but you gotta remember, this is just a 'coach' ticket ride." They both laughed and the attendants closed the ambulance doors. The unit sped away across the hauntingly quiet ramp. A small bus was there to take the rest of the passengers to a receiving area.

One was a particularly emaciated girl who looked to be about sixteen; she broke from the line getting on the bus. She ran straight toward Innkeeper and, to his absolute surprise, she threw her arms around his neck and gave him the biggest hug. Through eyes brimming with tears of joy, she simply said, "Thank you." One more hug and she ran to the bus and through its open door.

"Well," Innkeeper said, "I guess that's about the sweetest thing that happened to me today."

Dave Blaine climbed out of the rear seat of a plain blue, four-door sedan. Only the license number gave away the fact that it was a U.S. Air Force staff car. They walked directly to where Innkeeper was standing. "Well, you guys have done it again," Blaine remarked. "I never cease to be amazed at what you can do on such a limited budget."

"Yes Sir, we do our best," Innkeeper said, with a salute.

Jed looked at Innkeeper. "How bad is Mountain Man?"

Innkeeper winced and said, "Honestly, he'll be lucky to keep that leg."

Jed shook hands with the Innkeeper. "Well, you did a great job, thanks."

Innkeeper smiled and said, "All in a day's work, I just appreciate the chance to be back in the air again." The airport was still officially closed, and would be for another twenty minutes. As the last vehicle left to take the rescued hostages to area hospitals, Innkeeper and Blaine made their way back to the operations building.

Chapter Fifty-Eight
Back at the Canary

Many miles away, the Coast Guard ships had formed a small flotilla and were heading to the marina. The recovered boxes with files, computers and other items were stored in special containers that would be off-loaded without drawing attention. In the distance, the blackened hull of the Canary slipped silently beneath the waves.

*****

Waves lapped against a lone figure struggling to open the latches on the dull black container he clung too. Kim Rhodes smiled as he finally was able to unsnap the last latch. He was pleased with the shot he had made at the big man. As soon as he realized that the Canary had been taken, Kim exited the main part of the ship through a special passage way he had ensured would be constructed during the remodeling of the ship.

That passage way had brought him to a compartment just below the main deck. Within that compartment, he prepared his escape. He waited, watching the activity on the deck, waiting for his chance. When he saw the big man climb onto the deck, he decided he would make a final statement of defiance.

He slipped the .44 Desert Eagle pistol from his shoulder holster and aligned the sights on the unsuspecting victim. Braced against the edge of the bulkhead, he was invisible to any eyes that might search for him; yet was in a solid shooting position.

When he fired, he knew he had hit his mark. The big man flew into the air and his leg shot out from under him. Kim smiled and reholstered the pistol. He undid the latches that secured his escape vehicle, and once everyone had exited the Canary, he shoved it out. With the noise on deck, he knew no one would hear the splash, then he leapt into night.

Straight through the knee, he thought. *If he keeps the leg, he'll think of me every day for the rest of his life.* He had started to kill the man. He centered the sight on the bridge of his nose and the slack was out of the trigger. He didn't know why he had decided to let him live; maybe it was to prove how good a shot he was. He did hit the knee dead center at over sixty yards; at that distance, the target was the size of the end of a beer can. He felt no malice toward the man or the men with him. He knew they would eventually find him. He knew that as long as those men lived, he was in danger.

Eventually, they would meet again and he would fix that problem...the part about "as long as they lived." He now knew who they were; they were the ones responsible for Val's death. He now knew what they looked like; and better yet, they didn't know about him. They knew that someone existed, but their search for him had been unfruitful. If they had found him... he'd be dead.

As the ships begin to leave, the two halves of the container sank; leaving only a black Wave Runner bobbing in the ocean. Kim climbed on board and when the ships were under full power, he keyed the ignition and the motor sprang to life. He followed them at a discrete distance... for a while. The Wave Runner's tank was full and there were two extra gallons in a small tank, latched to the small vehicle.

After about fifteen minutes, he changed course and moved slowly, conserving fuel for the long trip back to the mainland. He continued to move silently north. At the right time, he'd beach the Wave Runner someplace. The night swallowed him up entirely and no one could hear the motor of the Wave Runner over the turmoil of other engines and activity.

It was as though he didn't exist.

Chapter Fifty-Nine
D-Day plus 2—Narrative

All members of the team, along with the Command and Control section, were finally assembled at Twenty-Nine Palms Marine Base; excepting Mountain Man and Nightingale. After two hours, they began to wrap up the debriefing. Blaine, Warlord, Psycho, Dogman, Jed and I, were at the front of the briefing room in heavy discussion.

The mission had been a success. A total of nineteen people were rescued from the Canary. The body count on the bad guys had climbed to thirty, and was expected to climb several more. The Canary had been sunk with minimal problems for the environment since the ship's fuel tanks had not been refueled yet. The cleanup operation would be called a "naval tragedy, the sinking of a ship with all hands on board."

The evidence found during the raid was being reviewed with a fine-tooth comb by the FBI and several other agencies. These included NSA, the IRS and several multinational law enforcement task forces.

Initial reports showed there was finally enough data to allow for serious prosecution of the principals. The Reverend Henry Mire had turned state's evidence and was singing like a rock star. He recovered from the electrical shock received from Madison and identified all of the contacts he had in Louisiana and the individuals involved in making the move to California.

David Blaine sat at a desk and closed the file. "All team members were successful in exiting the area undiscovered. We have a wealth of information that will lead to other arrests. All in all, I would say it was a total success, except for Mountain Man, and he is expected to make a recovery, although it will take a while."

Blaine added, "Nightingale has sent a report that I will now read to the team. 'Mountain Man is out of surgery and is expected to recover. He will keep the leg but will have to go through extensive rehabilitation. The joint replacement operation was simple in comparison to the reconstruction of the soft tissue.' Nightingale adds that she's been with him throughout the operation and remained with him in his recovery room."

He leaned back and smiled, stretching. "Looks like a good job folks. Now take some downtime. I think the TAC Team has done a great job. We knew this mission would not be as covert as the mission to Mexico. We are going to potentially have CNN, NBC, ABC, CBS and every other SOB crawling all over the scene searching for information. Therefore, the TAC Team will be on furlough until further notice.

"I want you people to go back home and relax. Stay out of trouble and get on with your lives. You have done a great job, but we need to let the heat from this one die down. Additionally, I think the back of the Corporation has been broken. We, you, have cost them millions; plus the political heat is really being turned up.

"The Reverend Henry Mire has become an embarrassment to his church, as well as the politicians who befriended him, and many of the local hoi polloi. Identified resorts throughout this country are being shut down, even as we speak. Our international contacts are moving on the ones we know about. That will take care of Kuala Lumpur, Brazil and the Middle East.

"Ladies and Gentlemen, it is time for the TAC Team to fade away until next time; if there is a next time. The Committee and I feel you have completed the mission," Blaine said, with finality.

"Well kids," Jed said. "It looks like this is the end of it."

I looked at my wrist watch. "Well, let's go out in style. I found a little microbrewery that has a barbecue waiting to be cranked up." Everyone agreed, and a small convoy headed out the gate of Twenty-Nine Palms and toward Palm Springs.

Soon, the pit was smoking and before long, everyone was eating. After a meal and a couple of drinks, the team members began to break up and head to their hotels to pack and return to their homes the next day. Eventually, everyone was gone

Warlord and I were the only two left at the pit. I pulled a cigar out of my pocket. "How 'bout splitting a victory dance?"

"Cuban?" Warlord asked.

"You bet, found some on the Canary," I said, as I put fire to the end of the cigar and took a drag.

Warlord took the cigar and blew a smoke ring followed by two more. "Very good," he said. "Hey Dad, what was it they used to say at the end of the Zorro show?"

In my best stage voice, I said, "...and when the danger had passed, Zorro faded away but the people knew that one day the danger would appear again. Then there would be a thundering, black horse ridden by a masked man returning." I finished with a flourish...

Epilogue

Abbu Nemiah was livid. Worse than livid, he was almost in the throes of a psychotic episode. Everything that he'd worked on for so many years was falling apart. In the past week, his holdings overseas had been raided and seized by foreign governments; governments that he'd spent fortunes on to purchase their cooperation.

His communications network had failed. He sat alone in the common little house, on the common little street, tucked away in a common little town. He hadn't slept in three days and was near exhaustion. His organization was destroyed, his financial empire was gone, and his power to influence others had been stripped away.

He sat at his computer, his last contact with the world that he had built. "So close," he murmured. "So damn close. All I needed was another six months and I would have had it all." Tears rolled down his haggard face.

His plans to shut down the corporation and move to his own island died before his eyes. The millions of dollars he spent to purchase the island and outfit it to serve his needs, were lost. Now, he sat alone and totally destroyed. The phone rang and jolted him. It was the special phone, the one dedicated for Corporation business. "Yes?"

"Are you alright?" He recognized the voice of Kim Rhodes.

With a calmness that belayed his tension, he said, "Yes, are you?"

"We must talk," Rhodes said. "I need help."

Abbu thought quickly and said, "Yes, we must talk but... Do you have paper?"

"Yes, go ahead."

Abbu gave directions for the place they would meet then hung up. He sat on the side of the bed for several minutes, letting the conversation he'd just had ramble through his mind. He hung up and dialed Hiram Jenkins' private number. "I am sorry for such short notice, it can't be helped. I have one for you if you can be here tomorrow morning."

"I'll have to make arrangements; I'll call you back within the hour."

*****

The next afternoon, Abbu Nemiah drove into the parking lot in front of the Home Depot in the neighboring town and parked. As he waited, he opened the bag on the seat next to him and withdrew a single syringe. Fifteen minutes later, a black Lexus pulled up next to him and the tinted driver's side window rolled down.

Kim Rhodes said, "Sir, it's a pleasure to finally meet you. After all of these years, it's my distinct pleasure."

Abbu smiled and said, "Kim it's a pleasure to finally meet you, although, as you know, I have seen you many times and followed your work closely."

"What are we going to do now?" Kim asked, seriously.

Abbu maintained his smile. "There is nothing to be concerned about Kim. Don't you know by now I have planned for every eventuality?"

Kim smiled and said, "That Sir, is what I wanted to hear. So you mean that we are still in business?"

Abbu shrugged and said, "Minor setbacks, Kim. Minor set backs are all we're facing. Let me ride with you and I'll explain what the next steps will be. Can you give me a hand?" Abbu opened his door as Rhodes opened his to help. A quick look around told Abbu that no one was paying any attention to them, and confirmed they were parked far enough away from traffic and bystanders.

217

When Rhodes stood up, Abbu shoved the syringe upward and injected its contents into the side of Kim's neck. The effect was instantaneous, and as Kim collapsed Abbu caught his weight and moved Kim back into the Lexus.

Roughly, Abbu shoved Kim's inert body onto the passenger seat and climbed in behind the wheel. Abbu started the car; once the door was closed, he turned his attention back to Kim and arranged his body so that he appeared to be sitting in the seat. After buckling the seat belt across Kim's body, Abbu patted Kim's cheek and said, "You are okay Kim. The injection will simply keep you immobile and compliant for a while."

Kim's eyes were intense and filled with fear, but he could not move or speak. Abbu said, "I want you to relax. Everything will be alright. In fact, things are about to become better than they've ever been." He patted Kim's face again and pulled out of the parking lot into traffic.

Back at the house, Abbu walked to Kim's side and hefted the dead weight. "Kim," he said, "I lied before, everything has gone straight to hell." Hiram Jenkins came out the back door and looked around, seeing no one.

Struggling, he and Abbu managed to get Kim up the back steps and through the rear door. Then they dropped him on the kitchen's linoleum floor. "I have to disappear and you're going to help me with that," Abbu said. "Luckily, you are not going to be missed and you can be of one last service to me. I need the loan of your body. This house is about to burn to the ground, with its lone occupant in it."

Jenkins removed Kim's wallet, substituting Abbu's. He then switched out watches, and removed Kim's necklace, bracelet and ring. "You are close enough to his build," Jenkins said. "In this small town, I doubt anyone will call for a full autopsy after this tragic event. Even if they do run your dental records, I've already confirmed yours don't exist."

Abbu sat down next to Kim. "I owe you an explanation; everything I have built has been effectively destroyed. I'm going to have to reinvent myself and start all over again. To do that," he said, as he stood up, "I have to die."

Hiram pulled a scalpel from his pocket and removed the plastic cover. He positioned Kim's face so he could see IT; that moment when life left the body. He smiled, a pleasant smile, and drew the surgical scalpel quickly and efficiently across Kim's throat. In one movement, he severed the carotid arteries and windpipe.

The only sounds in the room were Hiram's rapid breathing and the sickening bubbling sounds as Kim Rhodes drowned in his own blood.

"Now," Abbu said. "I have a few more things to do, don't I?"

"No," a voice said, from behind Abbu. "No, I don't believe you do."

As he died, Kim saw the big, raw-boned man standing in the door that led to the bedroom. He had a large revolver gripped with both hands.

"Who the hell are you?" Hiram said, as he spun around.

"Drop it!" The man shouted and Hiram let the scalpel fall to the floor. "Get over here next to your buddy."

Taking in a slow, even, breath the big man said, "My name is Ben Cochran. You and your people kidnapped and raped my daughter, Terri, and planned to kill her. I am here for justice." The big gun belched fire, and smoke and the .44 caliber slug tore through Abbu's head.

The big gun spoke again, and a slug tore through Hiram's left knee. Crumbling to the floor, Hiram lunged for the scalpel but he didn't make it. He saw the gun move to point at his head, but never saw or heard the shot that blew his brains all over the kitchen walls.

*****

Two days later, Cochran and I parted company for the last time. Cochran shook hands and said, "Thank you so much, but... don't take this wrong... please. I hope I never see again."

"Won't be any more reason to now, Ben," I said. "How's your daughter's recovery coming?"

"I think she'll be alright?"

"I hope so. It will take some time, but she has the time."

"She wouldn't have that time if you and the guys hadn't rescued her in Mexico. At least we stopped the bastards and I finally have justice for her," Ben said.

I smiled and said, "Technology is a wonderful thing. Thank Jed for that. Abbu, or Earl Levant, created his Cookie Monster years ago and it continued to work for him because no one knew to look for it. But other technology was constantly being developed and that is what beat him. Hiram Jenkins was just an evil bastard."

"I appreciate you letting me deal with them," Ben said.

"You earned that right and you evened the score," I said, putting my hand on the big man's shoulder.

"No," Ben said. "That score will never be even. But those bastards will never again do to anyone else's child what they did to mine. Am I going to have any problems with the law?"

"No Ben," I said. "As I told you before, you just had to exterminate some vermin. You did exactly that. Look on the bright side; if you had reacted any quicker, you might have been able to save Kim Rhodes. It would have meant his arrest and a media trial that could have gone on for months. Then the bastard could have had an opportunity to get out of jail at some time in the future. This is cleaner all around the board."

Ben and I walked across the parking lot and now stood with David Blaine, John Roberts, David Dillon, John Battaglia, Jed Kovak, Rich Leonard, Jim Townsend, Rand Leslie, T.K. George, Rich Leonard, Gregg Paul, B.J. Garrett, David and Frank La Borde, Marcus Caine, Zach Stone, Louis Davis, and Donny Three Wolves. Ben went to each man and shook their hand, one final and bone-breaking time.

"I owe you, all of you," he said, finally.

"Ben," Blaine said. "You owe your daughter a good life. Now get outta here and go make that happen."

Ben looked one final time at each man, then nodded once and walked to his pickup. He rolled down the window, waved and shouted, "If you ever need anything..." and drove back to his ranch and his daughter.

The TAC Team watched him drive off, then Doc said, "Okay men, let's go home. Remember, we're meeting next Monday at Mountain Man's place for drinks. He's out of the hospital and in dire need of some cheering up."

Not another word was spoken as the members of the TAC Team moved off toward their own vehicles and back to their own lives.

A Note from the Author

I first encountered Doc Roberts late in 1997 but it wasn't until much later that Doc really opened up to me. Together we crafted TAC Leader #1, What Honor Requires, for publication. TAC Leader #2, Night Hawks, is a chronicle of the TAC Team's second operation. Now that the information has been "released from governmental archives," the rest of their stories can be told. Watch for TAC Leader 3, RETRIBUTION.

Remember the opening narration from Dragnet? It was the story of Los Angeles Police Detective Joe Friday, "Ladies and gentlemen: the story you are about to hear is true. Only the names have been changed to protect the innocent."

In TAC Leader's case, the names have been changed to protect the innocent... and the guilty.

Visit us at
BobAndersonBooks.com

About the Author

Bob Anderson
Author, Speaker, Veteran

Bob retired as a Chief Master Sergeant from the United States Air Force Reserve with over 32 years of service. His last military assignment was in Iraq for Operation Iraqi Freedom. He served as the Security Force Manager of the 732d Expeditionary Security Force Squadron, responsible for a 221 person squadron located throughout Iraq, which included two law enforcement detachments and 24 military working dog teams.

Previously, he served as the Command Chief Master Sergeant of the 147th Fighting Wing at Ellington Field, Texas Air National Guard. As a Reservist at Barksdale AFB, he served as the Security Force Manager of the 917th Security Force Squadron, and as First Sergeant for the 917th Security Force Squadron and the 917th Medical Squadron.

As a speaker, his power message advocates doing hard things, especially when it's unpopular or uncomfortable to do so; simple and back to basics. He believes in unwavering commitment and courage. He believes success is earned, not given; it's a privilege, not a right. He says, "Excellence is the correspondent of failure—you cannot have one without the other. The attempt to eliminate failure will only eliminate excellence."

Bob holds PhD's in Human Resource Management and Safety Management, a Master's Degree in Police Science and a Bachelor's Degree in Social Psychology. His awards and citations include the Bronze Star, Meritorious Service Medal/3 devices, Air Force Commendation/1 device, Air Force Achievement Medal, Global War on Terrorism Service Medal and the Iraqi Freedom Medal. He is a member of the Air Force Security Forces Association, Air Force Sergeants Association, Air Force Association, American Legion and Veterans of Foreign Wars.

He is a qualified rappel master and holds a 2nd degree black belt in karate. Bob and his wife Pamela reside in rural southern Missouri.

Bob speaks on various topics including survival, leadership, and military specific training.

To inquire about having Bob speak at your next event, or to view other books published by him, visit www.BobAndersonBooks.com.

www.ingramcontent.com/pod-product-compliance
Lightning Source LLC
Chambersburg PA
CBHW032041240626
47154CB00003B/1025